THE
RISE
OF THE
RESISTANCE

PAUL ORTON

PROLOGUE

Every night, I think we'll get caught.

And every night, we somehow escape.

Sometimes, I imagine what will happen when they get us: what it will be like to be locked up. I remember how terrible it was being shut up in a house, and I shudder. What if I was stuck like that for years, with no hope of release?

I couldn't cope; I'm not that tough.

But I press on, regardless.

Millions of people already feel like that, trapped in their own homes, unable to get out. An entire country is locked down and we're their only hope. A group called the Collective want to keep it like that, so they can control everything. My mum and brother lost their freedom trying to stop them.

Somehow, I escaped, and now I'm caught up in the fight for freedom.

My name is Zac, and I'm part of the Resistance.

My name is Zac, and I'm scared as hell.

ONE

It's a grim night.

Kieran and I run across the field, wet mud sliding under our feet. It sucks at my battered trainers, threatening to pull them off, and splashes up the back of my legs. If we were doing something fun, like paintballing, this kind of terrain would add to the excitement. But instead it makes our job slow and difficult, crushing our spirits and tiring us out.

We jump a fence and carry on down a small path through some woods. My lungs are on fire and I need air.

"Stop!" I call, as loudly as I dare. "I need a rest."

Kieran draws to a halt and I notice that he's panting as well, looking beat. He leans against a nearby tree while I collapse on the sodden ground, needing to sit down more than I need a dry backside.

"I figure we're about half-way back," he gasps.

I nod, wishing we were a lot further than that. "Let's hope this isn't a route we need to do too often."

"True. This is the longest yet."

As runners, it's our job to fetch and carry, to drop off and collect things for the Resistance. Vehicles attract way too much attention, and it's difficult to move them around without getting stopped by the police or at roadblocks, so most Resistance business that can't take place on the Net is carried out on foot.

That's where Kieran and I come in. We do most of the actual running, as the youngest members. I never used to be fit, spending my free time slouched on a sofa playing video games. But over the last five months, we've been running the routes, clocking up more miles every night.

Tonight, though, I'm struggling. They've given us a stupidly long route to a nearby town. It's over ten miles each way, more if you factor in the difficulties of navigating the footpaths that zigzag through farmers' fields and the need to jump ditches and climb fences in the dark. It's hard going because we had to make our way there over uneven and muddy ground, in relentless drizzle.

"Couldn't they have waited until it was dry?" I complain.

"You know what Layla's like," Kieran says. He puts on a high-pitched voice, mimicking the Resistance leader: "It needs doing right now! It's urgent! If you don't pick up this package, then we're all doomed and the world will explode!"

I laugh. "Don't let her hear you saying that. You'll be back on kitchen duty for a month."

"If I have to slave in that kitchen again with Del shouting at me every five minutes, I swear I'll quit the Resistance and join the Collective."

He's kidding, of course. We can't quit. We have nowhere else to go. Except the streets. That would end up with us getting arrested; both of us are wanted criminals.

"Water?" asks Kieran, taking a swig from his flask.

I nod and he throws it at me.

That would have been weird last year, before everything changed. We used to be so paranoid about sharing germs and social distancing that we'd never dream of sharing a water bottle. Now, things are different.

In normal society, everyone is still afraid of the virus. No-one is allowed out of their house unless they have a pass and wear a full hazmat suit. All food and supplies get delivered directly to people's doors. All socialising is over the phone or the Net.

But the Resistance don't operate like that. They can't. I thought maybe they were taking temp-shots, which prevent you from being infected for a few weeks at a time. But temp-shots are in high demand for the rich and the vulnerable, and hard to get hold of.

So, we take our chances. To be fair, the Resistance don't have any visitors. And even when me and Kieran go on a mission, we don't visit other people; we always pick stuff up from a neutral location. That keeps the risk low.

Kieran looks down at me, shining his torch on my feet. My trainers are wrecked, ripped, and covered in mud. "You need new shoes, bro."

"Tell me about it."

They're the only thing I have from my life

before the Resistance, but they're falling to pieces. Even though I'm small for my age, I've almost outgrown them, but it's hard to get new stuff delivered to a secret headquarters that looks to everyone else like an abandoned pub. We can hardly place an online order, and Kieran and I have no money. We own nothing, not even the clothes we wear.

I take another swig of water. "We need to get moving. I hope this was worth it."

"It's probably just Layla's idea of a joke. Let's send the boys on a twenty-mile run in the rain. It'll do them good and keep them out of the way."

"I don't think even Layla's that harsh."

"Fair," allows Kieran. "Besides, she seemed particularly stressy about this parcel, even by her standards."

Layla had made it clear that failure was not an option. She'd told us that if we came back without the package, she'd send us straight out again, however tired we were and whatever excuses we had.

Don't get me wrong: Layla isn't horrible. Not really. She just has a lot to deal with. As the leader of our branch of the Resistance, she makes all the decisions. And it's only because she's cautious, and pushy, and driven, that things get done. I'm only annoyed because when you're shattered and soaked to the skin and your feet hurt, you don't feel too charitable towards anyone who's warm and dry.

I force myself to stand up. "Five more miles and we're done for the night," I say, trying to sound positive.

"I'm gonna sleep well tonight," says Kieran. "I hope we get a night off tomorrow."

"Yeah, right. Like that's gonna happen."

We jog along the dark path through the woods, lost in our own thoughts.

And the rain keeps falling.

TWO

We're jogging along a country lane when we see a flash of headlights in the distance.

"Where do we hide?" I ask, looking around frantically.

"Under the hedge." Kieran dashes over and drops to his stomach, edging under the bush. "Ew."

"What's up?"

"Let's just say that it's a bit muddy down here."

The car is getting closer. I dive on to the ground. Kieran isn't exaggerating. I'm lying in freezing cold mud an inch deep. It smears my face as I pull my body under the thorny branches. It doesn't smell that great, either.

We may be cold and uncomfortable, but at least we're out of sight and that's all that matters.

The car goes past, oblivious to us lying there.

Getting back out is torture. The branches scratch my back and snag on my clothing, ripping an enormous hole in my combat shorts. "Aw, man."

My hands and legs slip and slide for grip as I get to my feet. Kieran stands up next to me, his body dripping with muck like some kind of monster from an old-school horror movie.

I swear under my breath.

"I second that," whispers Kieran, shivering.

Our teeth chatter as we grab the backpack and start running again. Filthy water drips from my hair, onto my face. Trying to wipe it off is pointless when my hands are as dirty as everything else. Hopefully, the rain will wash off the worst.

"You know what, Kieran?" I say as we jog along.

"What?"

"When we get back, it's about time you took a shower."

"You're a funny boy," he retorts. "But you know I only shower on Tuesdays."

"That's what I'm worried about."

"Besides," he adds, flashing me a wicked smile, "that ditch was cleaner than Del's bathroom."

"True."

Whatever happens, I always feel better when me and Kieran do things together.

We're tight, like brothers.

The first signs of dawn are on the horizon as we run through dark lanes. We're relieved when we find ourselves on the edge of town.

Almost there.

But we need to be more careful now; there are houses. Someone might hear and report us. At least we aren't that far from the pub.

A few times, we've got close to getting caught. One time, I nearly broke my leg by jumping off a high wall when we had to run from the police. I had to limp back and use crutches for a week while the swelling went down.

Now, if we complete a run without being seen or getting injured, I chalk it up as a win.

The shops we pass are boarded up and abandoned. No-one uses them anymore; they're eerie and desolate, the ruins of a forgotten time. We turn off Bayliss Road into the car park of a deserted pub, sneaking around the back to a hatch that takes us down to a dark cellar. The first time we arrived here, we'd been terrified of what might be waiting for us inside. Now we're in and out of this hatch every night. It's the only way to access the Resistance headquarters.

We climb down the ladder. Kieran takes a torch from his backpack and guides us to the wooden door. We step through, letting it close behind us. There's a slight clang as metal bars descend, trapping us in a cage. It's a standard part of the Resistance security system.

A light comes on, revealing a staircase on the other side of the bars. Standing at the top is Del, the biggest guy in the Resistance. His beard extends to his waist and his long unkempt grey hair hangs down past his shoulders. He has the arms of a weightlifter and legs the size of tree trunks. You don't mess with Del; he's old-school. But he's a nice guy underneath it all, unless he's had too much drink. And tonight, he can barely walk.

"Wha' time d'ya call this?" he demands, lumbering down the stairs towards us. He nearly loses his footing more than once.

"Dunno," says Kieran, annoyed. "But we've had to run over twenty miles and we're covered in filth, so do you think you could let us through?"

Del chuckles as he gets close enough to see. "Did yer get wha' Layla sent ya for?" he asks, slurring his words. I wonder if he's been told to only let us in if we have it.

"Yeah, we got it." Kieran passes him the backpack between the bars.

Del looks inside. "Good boys."

I resent being called a boy. I might only be thirteen but I'm doing the work of a Resistance fighter. Still, it's pointless complaining. Del says what he wants. He'll never change.

I shiver in the cold basement. "Come on, Del, let us in. We're freezing and we need to shower."

"You be wantin' to use ma bathroom I'm guessin'?" he asks, leaning on the wall for support. "Dunno if I wan' you's in there in tha' state."

"We have to," pleaded Kieran. "Else we'll get hypothermia."

"I guess." Del shrugs and heads back up the stairs. "You can use it, but you clean it up after yer selves, ya hear me?"

"Yeah, we hear you," says Kieran.

"Sure. That's fair," I lie. Del never cleans his bathroom, so I don't see why we should.

Del reaches the top of the stairs and types a code into the keypad. The bars lift and we kick off our mud-soaked trainers and trudge up to the pub, our socks leaving wet footprints on the stone steps.

"Hardly a hero's welcome," I mutter to Kieran, seeing the deserted bar area. Everyone has already gone to bed.

"I'm sure they'll thank us tomorrow," he replies. "They'll give you a huge shiny medal and promote you to being a general or something."

"I doubt it, but maybe Trix will give you a kiss?" I tease.

"Maybe." He punches me on the shoulder. "That, my friend, is why I need to get clean."

THREE

I wake up, warm and comfortable in my safe place: a booth in the corner of the pub. I'm lying on one of the long benches, wrapped in a sleeping bag. There are quiet conversations and the click-clacking of computer keyboards, but I'm not ready to face the world. I plan to lie there for another hour or two, drifting in and out of consciousness.

But Kieran is sitting nearby, and he's getting impatient. He sees me stir and nudges my head with his green-socked foot. "Time to wake up, sleepy-head."

I open my eyes and see him sitting on the seats opposite, his arm around Trix, her as pale as he is black. Both of them are smiling.

"Hey, cut it out," I complain, closing my eyes

in the hope I can return to my dreamlike state, but Kieran shoves his foot in my face again, then uses it to ruffle my hair. "Sorry, bro. Can't allow it. Layla wants to talk to you."

"Was she up until four?" I'm annoyed and I say it with feeling.

"Calm it," warns Trix, pushing aside her long dark fringe and glancing around. "You know what she's like."

I sigh. She's right. If I speak to Layla like that, I'll regret it. The Resistance aren't cruel like the gang I'd once been forced to work for, but they're not soft either. There are always jobs that no-one wants to do. If you do something wrong or speak out of turn, you get the worst of them.

I stretch, yawn, and sit upright. I slowly pull my legs out of the sleeping bag and tug on some clothes. Kieran and I have two sets each. Mine are all cut up so the large camo gear fits my skinny body. The arms have been taken off the t-shirts and the bottom of the legs off the trousers. Long green army boot-socks are bunched around my ankles. It's a weird look, but I've gotten used to it. Everyone else in the Resistance wears old army clothing, so it doesn't seem out of place.

"How you feeling?" asks Kieran.

"Shattered. Like I've run a marathon."

"We pretty much did," laughs Kieran. "Twenty miles, bro. That's not nothing."

"Do I get that medal now?" I ask, with a half-smile.

"Better. You get breakfast." He calls through to the kitchen. "Del! Zac's ready for some food."

"I bet," says Del, gruffly, sticking his head out of the pub kitchen and looking in our direction. "It'll be out in a minute."

Moments later, a plate of mostly burnt breakfast is deposited roughly on the table.

"Thanks," I say, a little disappointed, but not wanting to complain. Del is not someone you want to upset.

"Don't forget, you boys are cleanin' ma bathroom later," Del says. "There's still muck all over t' floor."

"Sure, ok," I say, pulling a face at Kieran as Del walks away. "Looks like he remembered."

"Yeah, he woke up with a hangover and laid into me about the way we left it last night," grins Kieran. "He was in a foul mood, so I told him it was all your fault."

Del wouldn't have believed him. Kieran loved joking around, and most of what he said was just banter.

I demolish the breakfast, cutting the blackened sausage into small pieces. "What's bugging Layla? Anything I need to worry about?"

"I guess you'll find out. But I doubt it's good news. Hope you're not in *too* much trouble." He grins again, enjoying my discomfort.

"Ignore him, Zac," says Trix. "He's just teasing. It's probably nothing."

I finish the breakfast while Kieran and Trix do annoying couple things, whispering to one another, giggling and making strange noises.

I slip out from the booth. "Don't mind me. I guess I'll just go and find Layla."

Kieran glances up. "Good luck, bro. Hope she's not too harsh on you."

"I haven't done anything," I point out. "I'm not in any trouble."

Kieran shrugs. "Don't tell me that. Explain it to her."

I limp to the toilets on my way, my legs contracting painfully every time I take another step. I push open the door to the men's, bracing myself for the stench of stale urine which assaults anyone brave enough to enter. Del's pub was not a nice, clean, middle-class sort of pub, even before the lockdown. It was a neglected hard-core biker hangout. Hygiene was never high on the agenda, but now things are even worse. A lot of Del's biker buddies are in the Resistance. When they're wasted, they don't exactly aim carefully.

That's annoying for me and Kieran, who sleep in the bar area and use the same toilets. Most days, we have to put up with the stench as we wash in the cracked sinks. Today, the smell is particularly potent, and I step around a fresh puddle as I approach the urinals. This place badly needs cleaning, but no-one's ever going to volunteer.

I finish my business and wander over to the sinks, splashing water on my face and hair, trying to tame the bits that are sticking out too far. Before I joined the Resistance, Kieran's mum gave me a haircut, and it looked great, but now it's a mess again. Occasionally, one of the biker guys shaves it with clippers, but it's been a while since it was last done, and it hangs past my neck.

You need to get a move on.

Kieran's right: if Layla wants to see me, chances are I'm in trouble for something.

It's not a good idea to keep her waiting.

It'll only make things worse.

***

I pad up the staircase. In the distant past, the pub had rooms which it let out to paying guests. That's why most of the doors have numbers, and why everyone else has their own bathroom. Layla is in number 17, right at the very top. I stand in the dark corridor and knock.

"Come," she says.

I turn the handle and walk in. I've not been in her room before and it's the cleanest and tidiest place in the pub. It's hard to imagine it even exists in the same building as the crazy chaos below. The windows are boarded over and sealed so that no light escapes, helping to keep up the appearance of the pub being derelict. Usually, that makes rooms dull and dingy, but lamps keep this room clean and bright. A large bed is covered with a luxurious duvet, cushions placed neatly against the headboard.

In one corner is an immaculate wooden desk with a mouse, keyboard and three large computer screens on it, all the leads tucked out of sight. Two of the screens are full of computer code; the other one shows footage from the pub CCTV. I wonder if I've been caught doing something bad; it's easy to forget you're always being watched.

Layla is sitting in a large office chair and swivels to face me as I stand before her. She's a tall, black lady with a crewcut. Even in a chair, she's intimidating. I think she's in her thirties, but it's hard to tell. She always looks intense, as though she's concentrating on something. "Zac, nice of you to show." There's a slight edge to her voice.

"Sorry. It was a late night." I look down, embarrassed. I'm annoyed with myself for not standing up to her. She sent us on the stupidly long run, so it's her fault I'm this tired.

"You did well." Layla rarely says thank you, or gives compliments, so it catches me off guard.

"Thanks." Maybe I'm not in trouble after all.

"Sayeed also says you've been doing well in

your lessons. He says you show potential."

"He's a brilliant teacher."

Sayeed was given the job of trying to show me and Kieran the basics of how to hack. It's not easy for him. Kieran's not a great student, always joking around and getting distracted. But Sayeed has been patient with us and I've learned a lot.

Layla sighs. "You're still nowhere near as skilled as Trix."

That's classic. She gives a compliment, then takes it away. I don't care. I'm doing my best. "So?"

"I'm going to have an important mission for you soon, and you need to prepare for it."

"What do I have to do?"

"I can't tell you the details. Not yet. But you're going to need more intensive lessons, this time with Howard."

"Howard? Are you sure that's a good idea? Howard doesn't like... err.... people." I don't know how else to put it. Howard shuts himself away in one of the guest rooms and lays into anyone who disturbs him. Sometimes I have to take his food up and it's never a fun encounter. "Can't I learn from Trix?"

"It needs to be Howard. He knows more about computer security than anyone else."

That's true. There are several gifted hackers in the Resistance, but everyone speaks about him with awe.

"What about Kieran?" I ask. "We always do everything together."

"This is a one-man mission," replies Layla. "Well, a one-boy mission, anyway. Besides, I don't think it's a good idea putting Kieran and Howard in a room together for any length of time, do you?"

I can see her point. Kieran and Howard do not get on well. After their last fall out, Howard won't even let Kieran in his room.

"You're to report to Howard immediately. If you're not putting in maximum effort, then there will be consequences that will make kitchen duty seem like a holiday. Are we clear?"

"We're clear." The Resistance is hardly a military operation, but you still have to follow orders. "How long do I have before the mission? When do I find out more?"

"Less than a week," says Layla. "You'll be with Howard a lot between now and then."

"Great."

"And Zac, try not to wind him up."

"I'll do my best."

FOUR

I stand outside Howard's room and knock. There's no answer. I turn the handle and push open the door.

It looks like a room from the Pentagon. He has more computers than any person could need, with leads trailing everywhere. The room is dark except for the glow emanating from the screens.

The place also has a weird fusty kind of smell. Howard isn't messy like Del. He just doesn't think about anything that isn't on the screen in front of him. In all the time I've been with the Resistance, I don't remember him leaving his room.

He's sitting in his chair, tapping away, his back towards me.

"Err, Howard?"

"What?" Howard glances around, annoyed. He's a skinny guy with greying hair, much older than most hackers in the Resistance. He has stereotypical round glasses, making him look every bit the nerd. In fact, his face is distinctively rat-like. And he doesn't seem pleased to see me.

"Layla told me to report to you so you could teach me."

"You?" he says, peering at me. "No, there must be some mistake. She said I was to teach a guy called Zac. Send him up here, would you?"

"I *am* Zac," I say, annoyed that I've been bringing him food for months and he still doesn't know my name.

That gets his attention. He leans forward, making no attempt to hide the disdain on his face. "You? She can't want me to teach *you*. What are you, eleven?"

"I'm thirteen," I say, watching my tone.

He snorts. "Can you even use a computer? Other than to play games?"

"I know some stuff. Sayeed has been teaching me."

"Ha!" sniffs Howard. "Sayeed? Sayeed doesn't know anything."

I want to defend Sayeed, but it's wiser to keep my mouth shut, so I stare back at him.

"Well," he says, reluctantly, "I guess if Layla says it, then I have to teach you how to hack, however young or stupid you are."

"I guess." I wonder how many more insults I'm going to endure before this ordeal is over.

"Get me a coffee." He turns back to his screen.

"Sorry?" I wonder if he's understood what we're here to do.

"Are you deaf, boy? A coffee! Then we'll see what you know."

"Sure. Ok." I scurry out of his room and head down to the pub kitchen. As the youngest member of the Resistance, I'm used to being everyone else's scivvy. And part of me is relieved to have an excuse to get out of there.

But the relief is only temporary.

I can only take so long making him a coffee.

And then, I have to go back.

***

My first lesson with Howard is even worse than I expect. He makes me work for hours without a break. I sit at one of his many desks with a laptop, trying to analyse reams of code. He's asked me to spot the weaknesses and identify any loopholes. I usually enjoy this sort of stuff, but after a few hours, my head is throbbing.

"Well?" he demands, standing behind me, hands on hips.

"I can't see anything on this one," I admit, scrolling down. I'm so tired that the code is blurring in front of my eyes.

"You're not trying!"

"I am," I whine. "I'm just knackered, and hungry. I need a break!"

"No!" He bangs the desk with his hand so hard that it makes me jump. "No break until you find the problem with this code. We still have a lot to cover today. You need to focus."

"How long is this lesson gonna last?"

"That depends on how long you take," he declares. "But you are way behind. We have only covered half of what we need to get through today."

I groan. Our lessons with Sayeed only last an hour, and I've already been with Howard since breakfast. It must be half-way through the afternoon by now. "I can't go any faster. I'm trying my best."

"If you want to quit, you just let me know. I have better things to do than spend my time tutoring a whiny kid."

I'm tempted. I want to get up and leave. Howard hasn't given me a single word of encouragement all morning. He just demands things, corrects me and tells me how stupid I am. His negativity is grinding me down. But that doesn't mean I can just walk out.

"Layla told us we have to do this," I remind him. "I can't quit. And neither can you."

"Pity," he spits. "You're too young and too dumb for us to have any chance of getting you ready in time."

"That's not true," I shoot back. "I'm smart. I always got high grades at school. I learn fast. If I can't get this done, it's because you suck as a teacher!"

Surprisingly, he agrees: "That's my point! I'm not a teacher or a babysitter, come to that. Either crack the code or leave. I don't have time to listen to you moan." He sits down on his leather office chair and swings back round to face his own machine.

I grit my teeth and get back to work, wondering what I've done to deserve this.

It takes another half hour to find what I'm looking for.

I cough awkwardly. "I think I've found it."

Howard doesn't respond. He makes me sit there while he finishes whatever he's doing. I'm wondering if he's forgotten I'm there when he stands up and wanders over.

"Well, what's the answer?" I get the impression part of him wants me to get it wrong so he can have another go at me.

"There's a missing variable in these lines here."

He nods. "Good. That one was especially hard to find." It's the first time he's said anything positive all morning.

I decide to press the advantage. "Err, Howard," I mumble, "before we carry on with today's lesson, I think we both need a break. Can I come back in like an hour? I'll work extra hard, I promise."

Howard considers it for a moment. "Yes. That's wise. But make sure you come back. We have a lot to get through."

"I will. Thanks." I head for the door before he changes his mind.

"One more thing," he adds. "When you return, bring me some food. And coffee. More coffee. I don't know what a man has to do to get food and drink around here."

"Sure. No problem."

If Kieran was here, he'd have sarcastically bowed as he left. But that's why it was a bad idea having him in the same room. Howard isn't known for his sense of humour.

***

When I get down to the bar, Kieran and Trix are playing pool. I crash into a chair and rub my eyes. My head hurts from all the computer work and my body still aches from last night's run.

"Bro, you've been hours!" he exclaims. "What did Layla make you do?"

"She's trying to kill me," I moan. "I have to have hacking lessons with Howard."

Kieran's about to take a shot, but stops short. A broad grin stretches across his face. "Howard?

You're having to spend time with Lord Geeksworth?"

I nod dejectedly.

"That is harsh. What did you do to deserve that?"

"Layla says it's prep for some mission that's coming up. I don't have a choice."

"Sucks to be you." He turns his attention back to the game and pots another red.

"I have to go back up there in an hour," I say. "I don't want to. It's hell."

"Well, at least he gave you a break," says Kieran. He has no idea how bad it is.

"I had to pretty much beg for that."

"You'll be alright. You love that computer stuff. It could be worse."

I suppose Kieran's right. I'm being too negative. I need to view the whole thing as an opportunity. No-one else gets taught by Howard. It should be a privilege, not a new form of torture.

I'm starting to feel better when someone grabs me by the collar. I look up to see Del's angry face. "Where ya bin hidin' all day?" he demands. "Ma bathroom ain't gonna clean itself!"

FIVE

It takes ages to clean Del's bathroom.

Limescale, hair and other unidentifiable stains cover everything, as well as the foul-smelling mud we tracked in the night before.

"I don't see why we have to clean the whole thing!" says Kieran, for the fifth time. "We only added a bit of mud. It was already filthy!"

I almost vomit as I remove a huge wad of matted grey hair from the plughole. "I guess someone has to do it. Might as well be us."

"Hey, I'm Zac. Feel free to use me as a doormat," says Kieran, mocking me.

I shrug. "You know me. When you're my size, there's no point putting up a fight. You just get beaten up."

"Aw," says Kieran, pretending to be

sympathetic. He grabs me in a headlock. "Who would beat up a sweet boy like you?"

I roll around on the floor, trying to wriggle out of it, but it's no use. "Hey, stop that! We have to get this done! It's taking ages!"

"I reckon we've done enough," says Kieran, letting go of me and looking around. "It's in a better state than we found it."

"That's not saying much. We can't go yet. We haven't even started on the toilet."

"We didn't use the toilet!"

"Do you want to explain that to Del?"

"You can clean it if you like. I'll take my chances."

With that, he heads out, leaving me kneeling on the floor. I look around in despair. There's no way Del is going to be happy with it.

I curse as I get back to work.

***

I'm running late when I head back up to Howard's room.

I'm hoping he won't be angry. I have a tray laden with hot food and coffee. I've spent the whole of my break slaving away in Del's bathroom, but he won't care.

I knock on the door and push my way in.

Howard's sitting in the darkness, click-clacking away at his keyboard.

"I'm back," I say.

He grunts.

"I brought you food, and some coffee."

At that, he turns around, interested. I put the tray down in front of him and he snatches the coffee, gulping it down as if his life depends on it.

Then he turns his attention to me. "Sit."

I perch on the hard wooden chair, wishing it was more comfortable.

"Sometimes, computers are almost impossible to hack," he says. "When a network has its walls up, trying to break in can be a waste of time. Without access to professional software, you won't stand a chance."

"So, if I come across a situation like that, what can I do?"

"You kill them."

"Sorry?" I have no idea what he's talking about. "Kill who?"

"The computers, you imbecile. You have to

unplug them. Cut the power. Every machine is at its weakest when it's first switched on. If you can reset the computer, you can find a way in before the walls go up. As it boots up, you access the registry. Then, you insert a trojan subroutine. Do you know anything about those?"

"A little. Not much," I admit. I reel off what Sayeed taught me.

"Show me," he says. "Write some code that will provide a backdoor."

"Ok," I say, taking a deep breath. "I can do that."

I study the code on the laptop in front of me and get to work, much more focused than before.

It takes an hour to do it.

Howard comes over to examine my efforts, barely glancing at the screen before he spots a problem. "There's a syntax error. It won't scan. It'll give the game away."

I shrug. "One error. No big deal. How's the rest?"

He looks at me with utter contempt. He takes off his glasses, his eyes narrowing. "One error? ONE ERROR!?!? One error is all it takes to fail. If there is *one error*, it doesn't matter how good the rest of the code is. One error will allow them to track you down, to find you. One error will get you locked up for good! Is that what you want? To spend years locked up for terrorist offences because you mistyped a word?"

"I guess not," I admit, running my hand through my hair. "I didn't mean... I just meant..."

"You will start again, from scratch." Howard reaches over to the laptop, resetting the screen. All of my work disappears. "This time, get it right."

I bite my lip, forcing myself not to protest. It's harsh to have to restart from the beginning, but there's a reason he's the best at what he does: he's a perfectionist and won't accept any mistakes, however small.

"You need to understand there are serious consequences to even the smallest errors," he adds. "If you make another one, you will miss dinner."

That makes me sit up. "You can't be serious."

"I'm deadly serious," he replies. "One mistyped piece of code could cost you your freedom. It could cause you to fail the entire mission. It's not a minor mistake. It's everything.

If you're not willing to bet one meal on the quality of your work, you should not be willing to risk your life, and the life of others, on it."

I can't suppress it any longer. "That's not fair. Layla said I had to take lessons from you. She didn't say you could inflict random punishments."

Howard hesitates, then sits down at his own keyboard. "Let's ask her, shall we?"

He calls up a chat box: *Zac making mistakes. May need extra motivation. Suggest food is withheld for further errors.*

Three dots blink at the bottom of the screen as Layla types her response. I hold my breath.

Acceptable. Zac needs to learn. Use any means necessary.

"Use any means necessary. That seems pretty clear to me," sneers Howard, satisfied.

I slump back into the seat. "Sure. It's not like I have any rights or anything."

Howard is oblivious to the sarcasm. "Then we understand one another. Now, fetch me more coffee and you can try again."

As I trudge down the stairs, I can't help thinking that whatever I do will never be good enough for him.

But I have to keep trying.

It's going to be a long week.

SIX

When I stumble downstairs, my lessons over, it's gone nine o'clock.

"Kill me now," I groan, as I slumped onto a seat next to Kieran and Trix.

"Long day?" he asks.

"You have no idea. He didn't even let me out for dinner." I'd made another syntax error and Howard had followed through with his threat.

Trix is sympathetic. "Shall we see if we can find you any leftovers?"

"Sounds good."

The three of us head towards the kitchen.

"Zac, get us some drinks would ya?" shouts Del, who's sat at the bar with a small group of his biker buddies, playing poker.

"Sure," I reply. I nearly add "What did your

last slave die of?" but it would be a mistake. I fetch some beers from the fridge and take them straight out; Del isn't the most patient person when he has an empty bottle.

"Good lad, Zac," he says, ruffling my hair. I hate it when he does that.

"Anything else?" I ask.

"Nah, we're good."

I head to the kitchen where Kieran and Trix have put together a reasonable-sized plate of food. Kieran shoves it in the microwave and we wait until it pings. I grab it eagerly and pick at it as we made our way back to one of the pub tables.

"You're gonna need that," says Kieran. "We've got another mission in a couple of hours."

"You're kidding?" I'd kind of assumed that spending all day with Howard would mean I got out of any missions tonight. "How far?"

"Just a few miles."

That's good news at least.

"Is it raining?" I ask. It's hard to know what the weather's like because all the pub windows are sealed.

"No idea," he admits. "I hope not."

I suddenly remember that Kieran abandoned

me in Del's bathroom. "I still can't believe you left me to do most of the cleaning earlier. Great friend you are."

Kieran nudges me playfully. "It's nothing personal. I just don't like doing work. You're so much better at it than I am."

I grunt and take another forkful of food. There's no point falling out. He's my best friend, and that's the sort of thing he does.

"What have *you* been doing all day?" I ask, to prove I'm not sulking.

"Chilling. And teaching Trix how to play pool, as usual."

She laughs and punches him on the arm. "More like how *not* to play pool. I won more games than you."

"It's alright for some," I grumble. "How come I always have to do all the hard work?"

I'm envious of the fact that they've been relaxing while I've spent hours having one-on-one tuition with the grumpiest guy in the Resistance.

"Ah, poor Zac." Now Kieran ruffles my hair as well.

I choke on something and spit it out onto the

plate. It appears to be a piece of meat covered in hair. "Where did this food come from?" I ask, suddenly suspicious.

Trix and Kieran exchange looks. "It had been thrown out, but it was fine, and you looked hungry..."

"You got it out the bin?" I pull a face and push the plate away, wiping my mouth with the back of my arm.

"Sorry," shrugs Kieran. "We figured if you didn't know then it would be ok."

"Perfect. Just perfect. Don't mind me. Next time, could you put it in a bowl on the floor? To show me how much you really care?"

Kieran laughs. "At least you haven't lost your sense of humour!"

I aim a kick at him but the thick army socks cushion the blow and he laughs even more.

"Here," says Trix, checking no-one is watching. She reaches into her leather coat and pulls out half a pack of biscuits. "Have these."

I look at them, surprised. "You sure? Wait a second, where did these come from?"

"They're fine, honestly. I swiped them last night from Del's poker game. They were too drunk to notice. Suggest you don't let anyone see you with them, though. They might start asking questions."

I keep the packet on my lap, hidden under the table, taking one at a time and sneaking them into my mouth. "So, what's the deal tonight? Drop off or pick up?"

"Neither. Layla wants us to scope somewhere out. See what's happening."

"Really? Where?"

"There's a hospital facility at the edge of town, for people with the virus. But Layla isn't sure if it's real or fake. We need to find out. We have to keep a safe distance though, else we might catch Vicron-X."

"Sounds risky," I admit.

"We'll be fine," says Kieran, in his usual relaxed way. "We won't even go past the fence. We'll be using these." He pulls out a hi-tech pair of binoculars.

"When do we leave?"

"As soon as you've finished stuffing your face."

SEVEN

Kieran and I crouch behind a bush, a short distance from a chain-link fence. We peer through the leaves, trying to see what's happening in the hospital on the other side.

Lights are on in the main building, but the car park is almost empty; there are only a few cars and a couple of ambulances.

Kieran adjusts the settings on the binoculars. "I can't see much," he murmurs. "Someone just walked down the corridor, but they didn't appear to be wearing any protective clothing."

"That's weird," I whisper back. "In a hospital for virus patients, you'd think everyone would be covered up."

"And wouldn't you expect they'd have more staff?"

"Yeah. It looks pretty deserted."

Kieran stands to his feet. "I'm going in for a closer look."

"Wait," I hiss. "What happened to keeping our distance?"

"We can hardly go back and tell Layla we didn't find anything out. She'll kill us." Kieran pulls out some wire cutters and makes a hole in the fence, big enough to slip through. Then he throws his bag to me. "Look after this."

He creeps forwards down the grassy bank at the edge of the car park and steals across the dark expanse, moving from vehicle to vehicle like a shadow. I watch him sneak over to the main doors of the hospital, then hide behind a large sign.

Two security guards emerge from the entrance, doing the rounds. They don't seem to notice him as they walk past.

Not at first, anyway.

Just when I think he's in the clear, something catches the attention of one of the guards. There's the sound of raised voices as they make their way towards the sign. They've spotted him for sure.

Kieran tries to dash across the car park but he has no chance. The men are much too close, and one of them rugby-tackles him onto the hard tarmac. He's hauled to his feet and marched to a Portakabin office near the hospital entrance.

Now what?

They're bound to call the police or the Quarantine Agency and Kieran will be taken away. As soon as they take his DNA or fingerprints, they'll find out who he is. If he gets arrested, he's done for. His only hope is if I rescue him.

Move it, Zac.

I force myself forwards, creeping towards the security office. I don't know what I can do, but I have to try something. When I get to the cabin, the windows are too high to see through, so I listen through the thin walls. I can't make out what they're saying, but it's clear they're interrogating Kieran.

It won't be long before the police arrive and take him away. Maybe I can distract the security team and get them out of the cabin so I can sneak in and rescue him?

But, how?

I can only come up with one idea. It's a long shot but it might work.

Making my way across the car park, I check the car doors, seeing if any have been left open, but I'm out of luck. I try the ambulance. To my surprise, there's a click and the door swings wide.

The inside is stripped out and bare, little more than an empty transit van. Still, it's a vehicle, and that's all I need. The keys aren't in the ignition, but the vehicle is on a gentle slope. As soon as I release the handbrake, it rolls forwards, picking up speed.

I turn the wheel a little, directing it towards one of the parked cars. Then, I leap out of the driver's seat, back onto the tarmac, and scramble to a hiding place.

The collision is louder than I expect. There's an almighty bang as the ambulance smashes into the side of the car. The security guards rush out of their office to see what's happened.

As soon as they're out, I slip in to their cabin through the open door.

There's very little in here, just a desk and a couple of chairs. Kieran is handcuffed to one of them.

"Good to see you, bro," he says.

I rummage in the backpack for the wire cutters. "We don't have long," I whisper, as I snip the chain on the cuffs.

He leaps up as soon as he's free. "Let's move."

We bolt out of the security office. One of the guards is on his way back and he sees us.

"Stop right there." It's a stupid command, and he knows we have no plans to obey it. He sprints after us as we run up a grassy bank to the hole in the fence. Kieran pushes through first and I follow, but as I try to escape, the guard gets hold of my shirt. He tightens his grip, trying to pull me back inside the compound. Instead, I slip off the shirt and run away in my vest. He can keep it; I'm not hanging about. Thankfully, the hole we've cut isn't big enough for him, so he can't come after us.

Now, we're racing down the dark street, frantically checking we're alone.

"We need to get off the road before the police come," I gasp.

"You think?" asks Kieran. "Thanks for that brilliant advice. What would I do without you?"

"You'd be handcuffed to a chair."

"You're never gonna let me live that down, are you?"

"Nope."

Kieran grabs my arm and tugs me into the woods at the side of the road. "We can hide in here," he says, pushing through the undergrowth. My bare legs are being attacked by nettles. I pull the thick green army socks up over my knees, but it's too late. They already sting and itch like crazy.

We settle down next to a tree.

"My legs are killing me," I moan.

"Keep quiet," he urges, "else that'll be the last of your worries. We need to stay here a while until the excitement dies down."

Kieran only sounds that serious when he's scared. It's hardly reassuring.

So, that's what we do.

We wait it out, shivering in the dark.

EIGHT

Eventually, we limp back to headquarters.

By the time we get there, I'm shattered. Even though it's late, the bar is full of hackers and Resistance soldiers drinking and chatting. I won't be able to sleep for some time. I hate not having my own space.

Kieran and I sit in our usual corner and I push down my socks and examine the red marks.

Trix walks over and gives Kieran a kiss. "Looks nasty," she says, glancing over at the red blotches. "Hope you're not allergic to anything."

"Only stinging nettles," I say, drily. "Some of us don't have the luxury of trousers."

Kieran laughs. "Sucks to be you, bro. At least we got back ok."

That was true. The journey back had been

uneventful, even though it had taken us a lot longer than it should have done in our extra-cautious and over-tired state.

Kieran nudges me. Layla is approaching, the usual determined expression on her face.

"Well?" she asks.

"The hospital's empty," says Kieran. "Two of the security guys were talking about how pointless it was to guard the place when there's no-one there."

"And the ambulances parked outside aren't real," I add. "They're fakes, made to look the part."

Layla nods. "What we're hearing from other Resistance cells is correct. News reports of packed facilities and people dying from the virus are exaggerated, if not completely false."

"But people must still get the virus," I object, "else they wouldn't be taking people into quarantine and stuff."

"And the virus is real," interjects Kieran, suddenly serious. "My dad and brother died of it."

"It was," allows Layla. "It's definitely true that people were getting infected and dying in the early days, like your family did. But we're not sure that's still happening. The Collective may be using fake news to keep everyone in lockdown."

"Can't we tell everyone?" I ask. "Post a video on the Net or something?"

She sighs. "There are always conspiracy theories. We'd just sound like the people who claim that mobile phones caused it, or that the virus was sent by aliens."

"So, what do we do?" asks Kieran, frustrated.

"We have a plan. And it involves Zac."

I sit up a little straighter. "Ready to tell us what it is?"

"I suppose you deserve to know." She settles in the chair opposite. "A few days ago, a Resistance cell in London picked up an unencrypted communication being sent to a man called Aaron Greaves. Aaron is one of the most important people in the Collective, possibly its founder."

"The main guy, huh?" asked Kieran. "What did the message say?"

"It was a personal email, from his nephew Jamie, who's only just turned thirteen. Jamie is in real trouble. His mum got taken into quarantine, but he hid. Now he's home alone, and he's terrified. He's asked his uncle if he can stay with him."

"So, what?" I ask, confused. "How does that help us?"

"The Resistance cell in London blocked the message. They'll release it tomorrow, so Aaron will get it, but a couple of days late. We're hoping he'll agree to look after his nephew, and transport him to Arcadia. That's where you come in, Zac."

Arcadia. That's where the Collective operate from. I've seen pictures; it's like a holiday destination. Log cabins and treehouses set in a forest, next to a lake. The Collective live in luxury while the rest of us are locked down.

"You don't... You can't mean..."

"You're going to pretend to be Jamie. You're going to stay with one of the key leaders of the Collective, posing as his nephew, and find a way to give us access to their mainframe, so we can bring down their entire operation."

It sounds like the stupidest plan I've ever heard. I can't believe they're even considering it. "That doesn't make sense. Aaron will know that

I'm not Jamie. He must know what he looks like."

"That's where it gets interesting. It turns out that Aaron and his sister had a big falling out many years ago. In the email, Jamie says that he knows his mum and Aaron never got on, and that he's sorry that they've never met, but he's asking for help because he has no-one else to turn to."

"But surely Aaron will have seen pictures on social media and stuff?"

"Jamie's mum stayed off the grid as much as possible. No social media. No photos. I imagine that when your brother is a hacker, you learn to be discreet."

I lean back, trying to take it in.

"What happens to the real Jamie?" asks Trix. That makes me feel selfish: all I've been worrying about is myself.

"The other cell have picked him up. They're sending him up here to us so we can find out anything useful from him before you head to Arcadia."

"This is crazy," I say. "It'll never work."

Layla leans forwards, locking eyes. "It *has* to work. This is our best chance of getting into the Collective. Their computer systems are shielded.

We need someone on the inside."

"And were you going to ask me what I thought about this at any point? Whether I'm up for doing it?"

"That's what I'm doing right now. But you're the only kid in the Resistance who is the right age for this, who could pass as Jamie, and who might have a chance of hacking into their systems. We're all depending on you."

"So, I don't really have a choice." I stare at the table. Here I was again, being used. "Is this why I have to spend so much time with Howard?"

"We need your hacking skills to be up to scratch. We only have a matter of days until we expect them to take you to Arcadia."

"What happens if I get caught?"

There's an awkward silence. It doesn't help to put me at ease.

"No-one knows," admits Layla. "No-one has ever left Arcadia. We don't know what takes place there. But it's fair to say that getting caught is a really bad idea."

No kidding.

I'm about to tell Layla I don't want any part in this crazy mission. But she's looking at me expectantly and I've always found it hard to say no.

I take a deep breath and say the words she wants to hear. "I'll do it."

"Good."

I'm not expecting a medal, but I'm about to risk my life for the Resistance, and that's all I get. "Can we chill now?"

"As soon as we have some photos," says Layla, as if that's always been part of the plan.

"Photos?"

She looks at me as if I'm stupid. "There are bound to be photos of Jamie around his house; the Collective may go inside when they turn up to collect him. We have to replace his photos with yours before his uncle gets the email and has any reason to look."

"I guess." I'm too tired to think it through.

"Give yourself a good wash and come up to Room Twelve."

NINE

Sayeed has been busy. He's rearranged Room Twelve into something resembling a professional photography studio, with the bed pushed against the wall and a large white sheet hung as a backdrop.

He looks up as I enter. "Zac! Or should I say, Jamie? I hear you're something of a celebrity round here. I've been told to get some photos."

I shrug and shuffle forwards, nervous.

"Look," says Sayeed, gently. "I know you weren't expecting this, but we've got loads of photos to take so you need to work with me here, ok?"

"Sure, I'll do my best." Truthfully, I'm glad he's the one who's been chosen to do this. He's the nicest adult in this place.

"First, stand on the sheet. Right there in the middle. Then look into the lens."

I do as he asks.

"Perfect. I need a big smile."

He starts taking photos, moving the camera this way and that. He fiddles with the lights, making them brighter or dimmer. What I'm not expecting is for him to step forward and start messing with my hair.

I object. "Hey. What gives?"

"You have to look different in each shot. These photos need to appear like they were taken at different times. In fact, I'll need to give you a haircut."

I pull a face. "Tonight?"

"Afraid so."

By the time we're finished, it's past two. I make my way down to the bar.

Kieran's already crashed out in his sleeping bag. "Have fun?"

"Yeah, loads," I say darkly.

"You got a fresh trim." He peers at me in the dim light. "Not that it makes you any less ugly."

I snort at the insult. "Thanks."

"Cheer up. Arcadia looks like paradise. You

saw the photos: It'll be amazing there. Much better than this dump."

"I hope so." I climb into my sleeping bag.

For once, Kieran has a point. We've both seen pictures of Arcadia, and it is beautiful. I close my eyes and visualise it: log cabins and wooden walkways set between trees, the sunshine streaming through the canopy of leaves. After months scurrying around like a rat, it will be good to be out in the daylight. It'll feel like a holiday.

Provided nothing goes wrong, and they don't find out I'm not Jamie.

I don't even want to know what will happen then.

***

I wake with a start, coughing and spluttering as water splashes over my face.

"Hey, what the..." I sit up and wipe my eyes. Del is standing over me with an empty jug. "Did you have to do that? Couldn't you just have told me it was time to get up?"

"Boss told me ya need ta be wiv Howard right

away." Del shrugged. "Didn' wan' ya dozin' back off."

"What time is it?" I ask, slipping out of the sodden sleeping bag.

"Near eleven."

"Can I at least get some breakfast?"

Del's a scary-looking guy, but I know that deep down he has a soft spot for me.

"No time for anythin' proper," he says. "But ya can take a banana."

"Thanks." Beggars can't be choosers, I guess. I take it from the kitchen and eat it on my way to Howard's room.

"So, you finally made it," he says, as I push open his door.

There are a number of things I'm tempted to say, but I hold back. "Sorry." I slump down on the hard chair.

Howard seems satisfied with my insincere apology. "Layla says she has told you about the mission now, so you know you will need to gain access to the computer system in Arcadia. That will not be easy. Everything is likely to be password-protected and these people are not amateurs. You won't be able to crack their passwords. The best way to break in is to use special hardware."

"Ok." My head still hurts, and I feel the need to point out the obvious. "But where will I get access to that in Arcadia? They're bound to search me."

"That's not my concern. Layla will make the arrangements and you will at some point have a device. I've been told to show you what to do with it when you have it."

Once again, I feel like I'm trying to do a jigsaw puzzle that only has half of the pieces.

Howard shows me a small round piece of metal, the size of a small coin. "This is what you will use. It's called a copy-token. It's magnetic. You place it on the back of any computer, near the power cable."

"What does it do?"

"It records every keystroke that's used on the machine. When you return to the machine at a later point, you can access that data, and I'm about to show you how. Some of the very first keystrokes should contain login data, such as the username and password."

"But doesn't that mean that I'd need to get

access to a computer twice, not just once? That might not be easy."

"Again, not my concern." He doesn't care how tough I have it. "The tricky part of using this device is viewing and interpreting the data it gathers. You are going to practice on this computer." He points to a small PC, lost in the mountain of other computers, devices and cables spread around the room.

"Sure." I hunker down and get to work.

Howard isn't exaggerating when he says that understanding the data is difficult. It takes me a couple of hours to master it.

"I think you've got it," admits Howard, eventually.

"So, is that it? Can I go now?"

"Go?" Howard looks shocked. "Of course not. We still have a lot of other things to cover."

I let out a weary sigh. "I had a feeling you were going to say that."

TEN

At least this time I finish before dinner.

I'm eating with Trix and Kieran when Del strides over to our table.

"We're goin' wiv you tonight," he grunts at Kieran. "Big mission accordin' to the boss."

I look at him, shocked. "How many of us are going?" I ask, with my mouth full. Sometimes Trix joins us on our night-time escapades, but no-one else.

"You ain't comin'," says Del, turning to me. "You's stayin' right here."

"But why?" I'm confused: Kieran never goes on missions without me.

"Yer too importan' probly. I dunno. But there is somethin' importan' we need ya to do."

"Yeah? What's that?"

"Washin' up."

Kieran smiles at me. "Lucky you," he says.

"You can't be serious," I whine, but there's no point arguing. When Del collars you for kitchen duty you have to grin and bear it. Everyone is expected to pull their weight, especially as he does much more than his fair share of the cooking.

"Fraid so. I'll show ya's." Del grabs me by the shoulder and leads me into the enormous kitchen. Del knows how to feed large numbers of people, but he isn't keen on the clearing up part. I look with horror at the dirty pans, stacks of plates and bowls, and the greasy baking trays.

"You want me to wash all this?" I asked. "Who else is helping?"

"Jus' you on ya lonesome," says Del. "Everyone's on the mission or hackin' tonight."

"By myself? It'll take hours."

"You best make a start, then. Tough it out, boy!" Del smacks me around the back of the head. He has no time for slackers. "When I get back I expec' ta see this all sorted, you hear me? Else you'll be eatin' nothin' but dry toast for a week."

I sigh. "I hear you."

Chances are, it's not an empty threat, and I don't want to risk it.

I run the hot water into a deep sink and get to work. The dishwasher broke some time ago so everything has to be done by hand. I've been scrubbing greasy plates for an hour when Kieran and Trix appear.

"We're off," says Kieran, with his usual cheerful tone. "Wish us luck."

"You already have too much luck," I say, bitterly. "I get all the grimy jobs. Have you seen the amount I have to do?" I gesture to the other side of the kitchen where an enormous pile of pots and pans are still waiting to be cleaned.

"At least you're safe," offers Kieran. "No risk of you getting caught here, is there?"

"Getting caught doesn't seem like such a bad deal right now," I moan. "I bet prison would be better than spending hours every day slaving away in this place while everyone else does fun stuff."

"You don't mean that," says Trix, putting her hand on my shoulder. "It's one night. Don't take it to heart. We'll be back before you know it."

"Sure. Whatever." I'm not really angry with her. Trix spends most of here time stuck in the pub hacking. She probably feels left out when Kieran and I go on missions together. I haven't thought about it before. "Where are you going, anyway?"

"We have to fetch Jamie," says Kieran. "The Resistance cell in London have sent him up in a truck, hidden in a crate or something, and we have to collect him from a lay-by. The lorry is gonna pull in and the driver's gonna take a waz. While he's gone, we pop the back of the lorry open and get Jamie out."

"The driver's in on it?"

"Must be. But Jamie is not going to be a happy boy. He's been kidnapped and packed in a crate for hours. He's not likely to come quietly. That's why we need Del and the guys to help us carry him."

"All the way back here? On foot?"

"No, they're taking Del's Land Rover," says Trix. "We're running there separately. In case either of us gets caught."

"Sure you don't want to swap?" I ask. "You don't know how much fun you're gonna miss right here in this kitchen."

Kieran slaps me on the shoulder. "Nah, bro, you're ok. But do us a favour will you?"

"What?" I ask, stupidly.

"Rustle up a little snack for when we get back."

I throw a wet dishcloth at him as he and Trix dash out of the kitchen, laughing.

***

It takes me hours to get everything clean and put away. I stand back and look around. Even Del can't find fault with the kitchen now. The front of my t-shirt and shorts are both damp but they'll soon dry. I've finished: that's what matters.

I wander into the bar. A few hackers sit at tables, tapping away on computers. I rarely talk to them, especially when they're working. In the far corner, Sayeed is sitting with his laptop. He calls me over.

"Not on the mission tonight?" he asks.

"Nah, I had to do the washing up." I slump into the seat next to him.

Sayeed looks at me with sympathy. "It must be hard, living here like this. It's not how I'd have wanted to spend my teenage years."

I shrug. "Beats prison, I guess."

He laughs. "You're pretty cool, you know that?"

I'm not sure what to make of that, especially as Sayeed is something of a nerd, but I don't get enough compliments nowadays and I'll take what I can get. "What are you working on?"

"Take a look." Sayeed twists around his laptop so I can see the screen. To my surprise, it shows a photo of me wearing a school uniform I've never seen before. "I've been editing the photos I took of you onto ones that the Resistance found at Jamie's house. The other cell will print these off and put them in the frames and no-one will ever know the difference."

He opens a folder: images of me wearing clothes I don't own and in places I've never been. In a few of them, I appear a lot younger.

"How did you do that?" I ask, a bit freaked out to see my seven-year-old face.

"I have software that can age you forwards and backwards," explains Sayeed. "The great thing is, it doesn't even matter if you looked like that or not. As long as the photos are consistent when

Aaron or his people see them."

"Even I wouldn't know that wasn't me," I admit. "But are you really sure Aaron Greaves won't have any clue what his nephew looks like?"

"We've checked the Net thoroughly. There's nothing on there. No photos. No trace of him at all. His mum did a great job of keeping him off grid. You have nothing to worry about."

He's only trying to help, but he's not the one who's about to head into the viper's nest. And I'm not going to stop worrying any time soon.

I wish I was staying here, like Kieran and Trix.

But looking at the photos gives me an idea.

"Sayeed, can I ask you for a favour?"

"Always."

"It's just for a joke, but do you have any photos of Kieran?"

ELEVEN

It isn't long before the team return from their mission. One of the bikers has a boy slung over his shoulder. The poor lad has his hands and feet tied together with industrial tape. I can't see his face as he has a black canvas hood over his head, but I'm guessing his mouth is taped shut as well, judging from the muffled noises. He's carried to the men's toilets while Kieran and Trix join me at our usual table.

"You found him ok?" I ask. "Everything went well?"

"Yeah, no sweat," shrugs Kieran. "Poor kid. They crammed him in a tiny box. He has no clue what's going on; he's terrified."

It isn't like Kieran to show sympathy.

"What's the plan now?"

"I dunno. Keep him locked up here, I guess. Until you've finished your mission and we can let him out. It would be a bit of a disaster if he showed up at Arcadia while you were pretending to be him."

"Yeah, but..." I trail off in mid-sentence. This mission could take weeks. Jamie could spend all that time as a prisoner. He has it even worse than me. It's hard not to feel sorry for him.

Del's mate emerges from the men's toilets and calls over to us. "You lads need to use the women's toilets from now on."

I grimace. I'd assumed they were taking him to relieve himself. "They can't leave him in there. It's horrible."

"Nowhere else to put him," points out Kieran. "All the other rooms are being used for stuff. At least he can go if he needs to."

"This isn't right," I say quietly.

Kieran doesn't seem too happy about it either. "It's above our paygrade. We can chat to Layla tomorrow. He'll have to cope for now."

I remember how terrified I'd been when I was captured by the gang and chained up in a warehouse. "Has he had anything to eat or drink?"

"No," replies Kieran. "We had to tape his mouth shut to keep him quiet."

"I'm gonna take him something."

"Layla might not want..."

"I don't care." I say it with such force, I surprise myself. "We're not gonna let him starve. We can't ask Layla right now and he's bound to be hungry and thirsty. If Layla wants to punish me for feeding him, I'll take that risk."

Trix looks up. "I'm impressed."

"Why?"

"You never break the rules, Zac," she says. "You must feel strongly about this."

"Some things are right or wrong, and this is one of them. We're not terrorists and we have to do the decent thing."

Kieran grins. "Yes, Zac. You go for it!"

That should be encouraging. But, when he tells you to do something, you know it's a really bad idea.

***

I push open the door of the men's toilets.

I'm holding a plate of sandwiches and a cup of water.

Even though I know what to expect, I'm still shocked to see a thirteen-year-old boy sitting on the floor between the cubicles and the urinals, his ankle chained to a pipe. They've at least removed the tape from his mouth. His eyes are red from crying. He wipes tears off his cheeks as I enter but he doesn't stand up or make any attempt to move.

He's wearing skinny jeans and a hoodie. It's been such a long time since I saw a teenager dressed in normal clothes that they actually look weird.

We stare at one another for a few uncomfortable moments.

"Hi Jamie. I'm Zac. I brought you some food."

He doesn't respond, but he glances at the food in my hand. I hold it out to him.

I press on. "You don't need to be scared. We're good people. Nothing terrible is going to happen to you, ok?"

Jamie frowns, not sure what to make of my words after being locked in a box, hauled around and chained up in foul-smelling toilets. He snatches the sandwich and starts wolfing it down.

"Zac, can you get me out of here?" he asks, after a few bites. His voice is higher than I expect. There's desperation in his eyes.

"Not right now," I admit.

Jamie finishes the sandwich before asking another question. "Where am I?"

I'm not sure what to say. Layla may want some things kept secret. "I can't tell you. But it's somewhere safe."

"That man told me if I made any noise, he'd break my legs."

"Sorry about that. They want you to be scared so you don't cause trouble."

"But you don't?"

I shake my head. "I'm guessing you're a decent kid who doesn't even know what any of this is about. I got captured on the streets once and locked up, so I have some idea how you're feeling right now. I reckon you're scared enough."

Jamie swigs the water. "Do I have to spend the night here?"

"Afraid so," I confess.

Another tear runs down his cheek. I glance

around at the stained walls, the overflowing urinals and the wet tiles. I can't blame him for crying.

"How long have you been here?" he asks.

"About six months. Me and my friend Kieran arrived together."

"Did they capture you?"

"Not exactly." I think back to the first visit Kieran and I made to the pub. "But it took us a while to get to know them and trust them."

"Zac," Jamie whimpers, "what are they gonna do to me?"

"Nothing bad. They'll feed you and keep you safe."

I don't know if that's true. He doesn't look convinced either.

"You sure?"

"No," I say, truthfully. "But I'll try to make them go easy on you."

He doesn't respond.

Why should he?

***

As I emerge from the toilets, Del and his mates

are howling with laughter at the bar.

I wander over and see them holding a poster. There's a picture of Kieran on it. He looks younger than normal, but it's still clearly him. He's naked except for a dirty nappy. Sayeed has done a top job on editing the photo, just like I asked. Under the picture are the words "Kieran always likes to let someone else clean up his mess."

"Are you behind this?" asks one of the bikers.

"Maybe," I admit. "I thought it was time I got some revenge."

He lifts his drink, as if he's making a toast. "This is quality. Funniest thing I've seen in months. Remind me never to get on the wrong side of you."

"I'll second that," chuckles Del. "Yeh've got ya mate bang ta rights."

"Zac! You're dead!" I turn to see Kieran storming towards me. He's holding one of the pictures. "How many of these did you print?"

I grin at him as I back away. "Twenty. Or was it thirty? Thought everyone could use a laugh."

"Yeah? Well maybe they'll find it funny when I suspend you from the ceiling by your ankles and beat you senseless?"

"You'll have to catch me first." I dash behind the bar and into the kitchen. I glance back at him, trying to work out if he can see the funny side. "How angry are you exactly?"

"On a scale of one to ten, I'd put it around eleven."

"You do much worse things to me," I point out.

"Like what?"

"Like leaving me to clean Del's bathroom by myself. This is payback."

There's a stainless-steel counter between us. He leans on it and looks me in the eye. "What's got into you? First, you decide you're going to ignore Layla's orders and feed the prisoner. Then, you make fun of me, your best mate. Are you trying to make enemies?"

I realise he's right. Things didn't happen in exactly that order, but my frustration has built over the last few days and I'm fed up of being pushed around. "I thought it was time I stood up for myself. You say you're my mate, but you always take advantage of me."

That surprises him. It's his turn to back off. "I didn't know you felt like that. It's just banter."

"Yeah, well so are the posters."

He nods. "In that case, we'll call it even. For now."

"You sure?"

"As long as you take them all down."

"I guess that's fair." Now the danger has passed, I come out from the behind the counter.

Kieran grips my shoulder as we head out of the kitchen. "For what it's worth, I quite like this new rebellious version of you."

I look up at him, surprised. "Yeah?"

"For sure. But I don't think Layla will."

TWELVE

Kieran is right. Layla does not look happy.

She swivels around to face me. "You know why you're here."

"You're mad that I spoke to Jamie," I mutter, sullenly.

"No, Zac," shoots back Layla. "I'm not mad. I'm furious! You even fed the boy. What on earth were you thinking?"

"He was hungry. And he needed a friend." I don't feel like I should apologise.

Layla rubs her face with her hands as if I'm the stupidest boy in the world. "Did you ever stop to think that we might *want* him to suffer?" she asks. "If Jamie had spent the night hungry and scared, don't you think he'd be more likely to answer our questions?"

My cheeks burn but I hold my ground. "Torture is wrong. He's just a kid. He doesn't deserve any of this. And besides, he's more likely to tell us stuff if we're nice to him."

"So, what do you suggest we do now? Give him a massage, perhaps? Let him go home?"

"We could look after him better," I suggest. "We can't leave him chained up in the toilets for days. He could sleep with me and Kieran."

"And you don't see any problems with letting him roam around? Do I need to remind you what's in the bar?"

I shrug. "Computers. But they're all secure, right? We'll make sure he stays clear of them. And he can't escape the pub. Not by himself."

Layla pauses and goes quiet for a moment, as if performing some complex mental calculation. "We would need to keep a careful watch on him."

It sounds like she's softening, and I press my advantage. "We would. I'll talk to Kieran and Trix. We'll do it between us, I promise."

"It might take more than a promise." Layla tilts her head, thinking through the options.

"Whatever it takes. Just don't keep him locked up like that. What do you need from him, anyway? What were you planning to interrogate him about?"

"We need to verify his story," says Layla. "Check when he last heard from his uncle. There may be other things it's worth knowing: whether he's any good with computers and if he has any idea what his uncle is up to. We want to make sure that he isn't a spy and that we aren't sending you into a trap."

"You think that's possible?" I ask. My stomach makes a weird noise; I wish I'd had some breakfast, but they hauled me out of my sleeping bag and sent me straight here.

"We shouldn't underestimate the Collective. They're clever people. Who knows what they're capable of?"

"I'm pretty sure he's a normal kid. He doesn't even know why he's here."

"Would you bet your life on that?" Layla raises her eyebrows. "Because that's what you're about to do. We're sending you into the lion's den, and who knows what they'll do if they find out who you are, but it will not be pleasant."

I shudder. "I'll take my chances, if you agree to treat Jamie right."

"Fine," agrees Layla. "But there are conditions. You, Kieran and Trix don't let Jamie out of your sight, not for a moment. In fact, here's what we're going to do..."

***

I take another spoon of cereal, enjoying the look of disbelief on Kieran's face.

"She's not going to punish you? Even though you broke a direct rule?"

"Not punish, no..." I trail off.

"What are you not telling us?" asks Trix, suspicious.

"There is a sort of condition to Jamie being allowed out. And it involves both of you."

"What condition?" Now Kieran looks wary as well.

They aren't going to like it. "The thing is, Layla doesn't trust us not to get distracted, or leave Jamie alone."

"The woman has issues," says Kieran. "We can keep an eye on him."

"Wait," says Trix, cutting Kieran off. "What are you saying, Zac?"

There's no way to break the news gently. "The rule is that if Jamie isn't locked up in the toilets, then he has to be chained to one of us."

Kieran and Trix stare at me with horror, the same way I looked at Layla when she'd spelled it out.

"You can't be serious?" says Kieran.

"Afraid so. It's the only way she says she can be sure that he won't wander off and use any of the computers."

"But what's she afraid of? He's just a kid."

"She's worried he'll contact the Collective, or that he's some secret hacker that's been sent to spy on us." Even as I say it, it seems ridiculous when I picture the terrified boy in the toilets.

"Paranoid, much?" says Kieran. "Layla has been locked up in this pub for too long."

"Will you help me? The thing is, he can't spend time with me when I'm with Howard, so he'll have to stay with one of you."

"I guess." Trix doesn't look keen.

"When you say chained...?" Kieran asks.

"Your ankle to his ankle, only a metre apart. That's what Layla said. And Del has to keep the keys."

"What if one of us needs the toilet?" Trust Kieran to think of that.

"I dunno," I admit. "Guess you look the other way."

"Well, that sounds wonderful," he says, sarcastically. "Thanks for arranging that, Zac. It will be so lovely to be chained to a complete stranger all day while you toddle off to your computing lessons."

"What about when you're sent on this mission?" points out Trix. "What then?"

I give them an apologetic look.

Kieran groans. "So, just to be clear, you've dropped us in it. When you head off to the luxury of Arcadia, we're left looking after Jamie?"

"It's hardly fair," agrees Trix.

"He's a nice kid. We need to help him. Kieran, you remember how we felt when the gang captured us?"

Kieran nods. "Fine. But while you're here, I'm only looking after him while you're with Howard. After that, he's your responsibility. He sleeps with you."

"Deal," I say. I hadn't thought about how annoying it would be at night, but I'm not going to back out now. "Thanks."

THIRTEEN

At first, I thought I'd gotten off lightly when Layla didn't punish me.

Now, I realise that her new rule *is* the punishment.

After three days of the new regime, part of me wishes I'd left Jamie locked up in the toilets. It's not his fault; he's as frustrated as I am. But my situation is even worse than it was before, and that's saying something.

My lessons in hacking are also harder. The more time I spend with Howard, the more I hate it. Today he's teaching me all about code encryption, a new form of torture. After five or six hours, I stumble down the stairs, my head pounding from information overload.

Kieran is the bar playing pool, Jamie following

him around the table like a loyal puppy. He has to: their feet are joined by a long chain, heavy padlocks around each ankle.

"Hey."

"Hey bro." Kieran pots another ball. "Had a fun afternoon?"

"Could be worse I guess," I say. "You?"

"Not too bad," admits Kieran. "Jamie's getting a lot better at pool. But that's my shift done for today." He calls over Del, who swaps the chain from Kieran's ankle to mine. Once we're connected, we crash on one of the cushioned seats, side by side.

"So, how you getting on?" I ask Jamie. "Really?"

He yawns. "I'm still tired. It's hard to sleep like this."

"Tell me about it." Because of the chain, we can't zip up our sleeping bags. And every time we roll over, we wake each other.

"It's still better than spending the night in the toilets," he says, quickly, as if he's worried I might have second thoughts. "I'm grateful you got me out of there."

"No problem."

"It's just weird," he continues. "I mean you're being friendly and all, and so is Kieran and Trix and that, but I'm still being treated like a prisoner."

"I get that."

"I got to meet with Layla this morning. And one of the other guys. Once I answered all their questions, they told me what this place is and how you're trying to get everyone freed from the lockdown. It sounds crazy."

"So, you at least understand where we're coming from?" I ask. "And why we have to be extra careful with you?"

"Sort of." He looks at me, sadly. "But I'm not part of the Collective, I swear. I just happen to be related. My mum didn't like my uncle. I never even met him. I had no idea he was in charge of a global conspiracy: that's pretty hard to believe."

"Why did they fall out?"

"I dunno. Mum never talked about it."

There's one question that I've been meaning to ask for some time. "Why did you contact him? When your parents were taken into quarantine? I mean, how did you even know how to get in touch?"

He looks hurt. "You don't believe me, do you?"

"I do. I just want to know."

Jamie looks away. "It all happened so fast. The Quarantine Agency showed up at my house. Mum slipped me his email address, before she was taken. She told me he was the one person who could rescue me and that I should contact him."

He clams up as Del wanders over. "Layla wants to see ya," he says to me. "But this 'un needs to stay down 'ere."

I shout to Kieran. "I have to see Layla. So, you need to have Jamie."

Kieran throws down his cue. "So, I do like a five-hour shift and you do five minutes and then it's my turn again?"

I feel guilty but what can I do. "I'll try to be quick, I promise." I lift my foot so Del can remove the padlock.

"Fine, bro, but if you're not back here in ten minutes, I'm putting him back in the toilets." He catches Jamie's eye, a little embarrassed. "Hey, sorry, but a guy's gotta have some time with his girlfriend."

"Sure," says Jamie. "Or, here's an idea: why

don't you let me walk around freely? Like a human being?"

"You know why. Too many computers," I remind him.

"Haven't you heard of password protection?"

"You could be a hacker."

"A hacker?" Jamie laughs.

"What?" I ask.

"It's funny that you'd even think that. I'm terrible with computers. My parents hated me using them. When we had to home-school, I could barely switch it on without causing some kind of problem. Everyone used to tease me about it, like I was jinxed."

"That might not be such a bad thing." If Layla finds out Jamie is a bust with technology, then she might feel a little easier about letting him walk around. I'd prefer it if we didn't have to keep him chained up like an animal, and not just because it makes my life difficult. It makes me feel like one of the bad guys.

"I hope the meeting goes well," says Jamie.

"I'm not holding my breath."

Truthfully, meetings with Layla are never good news.

And I have a particularly bad feeling about this one.

***

I use the toilet before I head up, more from nerves than the need to go.

When I arrive in Layla's room, I'm surprised to discover Del is already there, having beaten me up the stairs. His tattooed arms, straggly hair and grubby clothes look out of place in the neat room. He's sits in a comfortable armchair, one boot resting on his knee, like a homeless person squatting in a five-star hotel. He and Layla are deep in conversation but they stop speaking as I enter.

As usual, there's no small talk.

"We have an issue," she says. "We need to get you to Jamie's house tonight."

"I thought we had a few more days?"

"So did we, but Aaron has been quick off the mark. He emailed to say he would pick Jamie up at 3am from the back garden."

"But Jamie's house is in London," I exclaim. "I'll never get there in time."

"Ya will if I take ya," interrupts Del. "With time ta spare!"

"But there'll be roadblocks and patrols and stuff?"

Del gives me a sly look. "Don't ya worry 'bout that. We 'ave a plan."

"We can get you there," agrees Layla. "But you'll have to leave at eleven, which doesn't give us much time to get ready." She turns to the old biker. "Are you sure you can arrange everything, Del?"

"Easy. They won't know what's hit 'em! Do ya need me for anythin' else?"

"No. Make the arrangements," says Layla. "Sayeed will aid you with communications."

"Alright." He turns to me. "You got the ride of ya life to look forward to!" Del saunters out of the room, grinning.

"You might as well sit down," Layla says.

I slump into the chair that Del has vacated. "What happens now?"

"We have to make sure you can hack in to the Collective network. Has Howard taught you how to use the copy-token?"

"For sure," I reply. "He's spent ages going over

97

that. He tests me every day; I could do it in my sleep. But where am I going to get one of those? I mean, they'll search me when I arrive, won't they? Isn't it risky trying to sneak it in?"

Layla pulls a bunch of paperwork out of a file and spreads it over the coffee table. One of the papers opens out into a huge map. I slide on to my knees to examine it more closely: it's a plan of Arcadia.

"These are some of the plans your mum lost her freedom for. They helped us to locate the Collective headquarters and they've also helped us work out how to compromise their security."

An extensive area of green woodland surrounds a blue lake. Hundreds of squares are scattered about, connected by lines. "Are these..?"

"All buildings, yes." Layla points at them with her finger. "The brown outlines show treehouses. The lines connecting them are wooden walkways."

"What about the black shapes?"

"They're other structures. Stores, meeting rooms, it's hard to be sure from what we have."

"It must be massive."

"It is. It's arranged into five hubs spread around the lake. Near the centre of each of them are communal buildings, surrounded by dwellings in the trees."

"And there are gaps between each hub?"

"We're not sure what the logic is."

"These two thick lines," I say, tracing them with my finger. "Are these fences?"

"Two of them, several metres apart, with no gaps and full surveillance. They take their security seriously."

My heart sinks. I've been wondering whether I'll get into Arcadia, but I haven't stopped to consider whether I'll get back out. "How does this help me sneak in a copy-token?"

"Look up here." Layla indicates a small blue line near the top of the map. "Arcadia is surrounded by large hills; this stream flows into the lake from higher ground. We're going to send something over both fences and it should land here." She points to a spot next to the stream.

"A drone, I'm guessing?"

"No. They'd spot that kind of technology in seconds. We'll use this." She reaches into a box and hands me a large grey pebble. "It has a secret compartment."

As I examine the stone, I spot a small indent. Using my fingernail, I'm able to prise it open.

"Genius," I say. "They'll never suspect there's anything in this."

"The copy-token will be inside. We'll catapult it over the fence to land next to the stream on your side."

I glance nervously at the map. "But isn't this green area all dense woodland? Won't there be hundreds of rocks?"

"Possibly," she admits. "But it's the only way we can get something over both fences without attracting attention."

I stare again at the map, feeling queasy. I'm leaving tonight, and the risk is all too real. "What if I screw up?"

"Then we lose our best chance at ending the lockdown and defeating the Collective. We'll try to get you out of there by using Jamie as a hostage, but who knows whether it'll work."

"Right."

"Zac," says Layla, grabbing my shoulders. "Do whatever it takes to get us access to their network. If you fail, it might be years before we get another chance. Not to mention what they might do to you if you're caught."

"So, no pressure?" I ask, with a weak smile.

"None at all." Layla gives a rare smile of her own. "Now, you need to go and swap clothes with Jamie. If there's anyone waiting for you at the house, you can hardly show up wearing those rags without raising suspicion."

I glance down at my grubby cut-off t-shirt and torn shorts. "He's not gonna wear this stuff."

"He doesn't have a choice," says Layla, steel in her voice. "Jamie's still our prisoner. Either you get him to do it the easy way or we'll do it the hard way. He'll like that even less."

"I'll tell him." I shuffle to the door.

In a couple of hours I'll be heading to London to begin my mission.

I wish Kieran was going with me.

But this is one mission I have to do alone.

FOURTEEN

"I can't believe you're making me do this," moans Jamie, stripping off his jeans in the men's toilets.

I pull off my torn, sleeveless t-shirt, and hand it to him. "It's not my fault. I'm just following orders."

Jamie examines it with a look of disgust. "How many days have you been wearing this?" he asks.

"You don't want to know." I pick up his polo shirt, catching a whiff of stale sweat. "Hey, this isn't all that fresh."

Jamie smiles. "At least it fits you." That was true. By the time I've changed into his clothes, I feel like a normal teenager for the first time in months. Jamie, meanwhile, has the raw end of the deal.

He looks in the mirror. "Aw man, this stuff is

so grim." He reaches down and scratches his ankle. "How itchy are these socks?"

"You get used to them," I say. "At least they keep you warm."

"So, what happens now?" he asks, leaning against the sink. "You get to pretend you're me, right?"

"I have to leave tonight. They're sending me to your house. Any idea how I get in?"

"You want me to help you break into my house? While I stay here, chained up like a convict?"

I can see his point. "We're just doing what we have to do to end the lockdown. And we need your help."

"I'm going to be stuck here for weeks, aren't I?" He looks at me in the mirror, resignation on his face.

"I've asked Kieran to take care of you," I say, avoiding the question. "He's a good guy. He'll make sure you're treated right."

Jamie's eye well up. "I don't want you to go."

I don't want to leave him either. It's weird how quickly we've become friends. "I have to. Will you help me get in to your house or not?"

After a brief pause, Jamie sighs. "I guess I might as well tell you. The Resistance already forced their way in the back door when they took me prisoner. It's probably still unlocked."

"Thanks."

"Anything else you want?" Jamie says bitterly. "Or do you have everything you need now so you can stop pretending you care?"

"It's not like that. Honestly, it's not." I put my hand on his shoulder and squeeze hard. "We just had some hard choices to make, and you've been unlucky. That's all."

"Yeah, right."

"Come on," I say, trying to push my guilt away. "We need to go."

***

Del and Kieran are waiting in the bar.

"Well, Zac got himself some decent threads at last," teases Kieran. "Give us a twirl."

"Don't be an idiot," I say, punching him on the arm.

"And Jamie here looks like a proper Resistance fighter!" he adds, grabbing him in a friendly headlock. Jamie can't help smiling and it puts me at ease. Maybe he'll be ok.

"I preferred my old stuff," admits Jamie.

"Dressed like that, we'll have you running the routes with us in no time," adds Kieran, cheerfully. It's not true, though. There's no way Layla will ever let Jamie out of the pub.

Del clears his throat and holds up the chain. "Touching as all this is, giv' me yer ankles," he says to Jamie and Kieran. "Ya know the rules."

"Sure." Kieran grabs a chair and places his foot on it. Jamie does the same while Del fastens the padlocks.

"You know what, Zac?" says Jamie. "I'm gonna be having words with Layla about this whole arrangement. It's not working for me."

"Good luck with that."

"Are you off right now?" asks Kieran. "Do we have to give you a hug and stuff, or do we at least pretend we're men?"

"We can pretend," I agree. "But if I die, you still have to cry at my funeral."

"Deal," says Kieran, and we bump fists, then he pulls me into a tight hug, anyway. "Stay safe, bro."

"He's not leavin' yet," says Del. He turns to me: "Before we go, ya have ta see Howard."

"Well aren't you the lucky one," grins Kieran.

***

I open Howard's door and cough, making sure he knows I'm there.

"Oh, it's you." He turns around, peering at me through his glasses. "Layla tells me you're leaving tonight. I've been working all evening to get the roadblocks lifted."

"You can do that?"

"It's not simple but I think I've found a way in."

"Del told me you wanted to see me?" I'm keen to get out of the musty room as quick as possible.

"Ah yes, I just wanted to say that teaching you has been an absolute pain, but you've learned a lot."

"Right." I don't know what to say to that. I'm not sure if he's congratulating me or himself. "Err, thanks, I guess."

"And I want to wish you good luck." Howard smiles as he says it. I've never seen him smile before. It makes him look years younger. "If you remember what I've taught you, then you should be able to hack into the Collective's system."

"I hope so," I say. "As long as I can get the device."

"Remember," he says, raising a finger, "no syntax errors."

I give him a weak smile. "I'll try."

"Check. Double-check. And then?"

"Triple-check."

"Good. Now, I must try to find how they've encrypted the traffic system or you won't be going anywhere." Howard turns back to his screens and is instantly lost in his world of code.

I trudge back down the stairs, feeling like I'm carrying a huge rucksack filled with heavy weights.

FIFTEEN

It's so dark I can barely see the others.

Del and his biker mates are dressed in motorbike leathers and I'm grateful I have Jamie's thick skater hoodie to protect me from the wind. We're in the pub car park, preparing for our long trip to London, but there's no sign of any motorbikes. They are carrying guns, though, and it makes me nervous.

"Greasy's crew are in," mutters one guy quietly—a large bald guy called Leo. "And the Tearaways are on board as well."

A few of the other guys chuckle. "Even the kiddies wanna play."

"I ain't been this stoked in years," says Del, stroking his beard. "This'll show 'em they can't keep us locked up like animals."

The last bikers emerge from the cellar.

"Time to move." Del leads us round to the front of the building and along the street, towards the row of shops a little further down.

"What's the plan?" I whisper to Del.

"First, we get our wheels," he mutters back. "But we ain't gonna be ridin' alone. There's gonna be bikers all over the country breakin' lockdown tonight. A mass protest."

"Sounds good." I can't help but be impressed that all of this has been organised so quickly.

"Wiv the cops so distracted they ain't gonna have time t' worry about me and you. We'll keep our heads down an' make it to London in no time."

My stomach tightens. "Won't they get arrested?"

"Some," shrugs Del. He gives me a lopsided smile. "The slow 'uns."

Behind the abandoned shops is a derelict row of garages. The bikers pull out keys and slide open the doors, rusty metal making loud grating noises. At this rate, everyone nearby is going to hear us, but they don't seem to care. The headlights and handlebars of several motorbikes gleam in the darkness.

"It's been too long," says Del, softly, shining his torch at a Harley Davidson. He pulls a helmet off a hook and straps it on, then throws a spare to me. I put it on, even though it's way too big.

Del slides his shotgun into a holster on the side of the bike and climbs on. "Get ya' butt on here," he says.

I try to straddle the seat behind him, but can't even get my leg over. One of the bikers laughs and hauls me up by the seat of my jeans, giving me a wedgie. I can't sort it out as I have to cling to Del for balance, my skinny arms barely able to reach around his waist. I'm already uncomfortable and we haven't even set off.

Del starts his engine and the other bikers follow his lead. The still night air is filled with the growling roar of motorbikes waiting to be released into the night like hungry beasts. Del looks around to make sure the rest of the crew are ready and raises his arm in a kind of salute.

The world moves as we shoot forward. I've never been on a bike before and I cling on for dear life. We zoom down dark roads, the others close behind us, some guys whooping and screeching. I want to tell them to shut up. Kieran and I have to sneak around when we go on a mission. But that's not the deal here.

"You's all ok?" I hear Del's tinny voice in my helmet. There's a comms system installed so the bikers can communicate with one another. I hear the other guys respond.

"Never better!"

"Yeeeeeeee Haaaaaaaa!"

"Man, I miss this!"

"They ain't gonna be stoppin' us tonight!"

The air feels a lot colder as the bikes pick up speed and I shiver in my hoodie, hugging Del as tightly as I can, wishing I could straighten out my underwear.

***

We're cruising down an empty dual carriageway when trouble hits.

The bikers are in a V formation, Del and me at the front. Over the roar of the bikes I can make out another noise: a siren. I glance back to see a police car closing in.

"The police," I warn. "They're after us!"

"Even in lockdown, nuffin changes," laughs one of the bikers. "But they ain't catchin' us on them wheels!"

"Time ta rip!" growls Del.

"Can't we let him get closer," suggests one of the others. "Just for a laugh?"

"Ain't worth the risk. Hold tight, Zac. Three, two, one..."

With an almighty roar, the Harley shoots forward at an incredible speed and I tighten my grip on Del's jacket. The scenery rushes by in a blur, and I try not to think about what it'll be like if we crash.

I don't dare to look behind us now, in case I lose my balance, but it sounds like the police car is falling further and further behind.

"It's almost too easy!" declares one guy. But he's spoken too soon.

"We 'ave a problem," says Del, grimly. "Eyes ahead."

I can see an area in the far distance illuminated by floodlights. Toll booths and large barriers block our way. Warnings flash on LED signs: "SLOW DOWN" and "CHECKPOINT AHEAD".

There's a lot of swearing over the radio. With the roadblock in front and the police behind, we literally have nowhere to go.

"Howard was meant to be sorting this," moans Leo. "What do we do?"

"Hold steady," demands Del, speeding towards the checkpoint. "We're goin' thru'."

"Del, if we hit them barriers we'll be killed!"

"I ain't makin' suggestions. I'm giving orders! Now hold steady!"

I glance sideways. A few of the other bikers are exchanging worried looks through their helmets. They're sure that continuing towards the roadblock is madness. For what it's worth, I agree with them.

We're hurtling at the red and white barriers at an unholy speed and there's no way we'll be able to smash our way through. We're going to die.

And before that, it's going to hurt.

It's *really* going to hurt.

SIXTEEN

It happens at the last possible second.

The barriers are so close, it seems inevitable that we'll crash. But what can I do? I can't jump off a bike going a hundred miles an hour. So, I do the only thing I can think of: wait for impact.

"Duck!" yells Del, leaning forwards in his seat.

I hunker down as low as I can, knowing it's pointless. The barrier will still take our heads off, and a lot else as well.

We're going to die.

That's what I'm thinking when the barriers lift.

There's a slight scraping noise as Del's helmet catches the bottom edge of the raising bar but we make it. The other bikers aren't far behind us but they easily get through as all the checkpoint barriers rise higher. The attendant in one booth is frantically pressing buttons, trying to get them back down.

"Looks like Howard ain't completely useless after all!" declares Del, chuckling. "Better late than never. Still, they'll be waitin' for us if we stay on this route."

"We'd better use smaller roads," suggests Leo, over the radio. "There's a shortcut through a town if we take the next turning. It should throw them off our scent."

"Aye. Agreed." The bike slows a little as we turn onto the slip road, then tilts as we reach a roundabout. I clutch Del's leather jacket, worried I'll slip off.

Fields and grassy verges give way to streets filled with houses as we whip through a town, curtains twitching at the windows. We're making good progress, but as we career down the street, I see the flash of blue lights. We're heading straight into a police ambush.

"Fall back!" yells Del. He brakes and whips the bike around so suddenly it catches me by surprise. I lose my balance, falling sideways onto the tarmac. The helmet bangs the road hard and pain shoots up my arms and legs. My elbows and knees are grazed, Jamie's jeans torn. Del and the other bikers don't even realise what's happened: they're accelerating away.

"Help!" I shout into my helmet, unsure if they can hear me. "I fell! I'm in the road."

I turn around. Headlights are bearing down on me, sirens blaring and blue lights flashing. I push myself up and wave at them, scared they'll run me down in their attempts to follow the bikers. I don't want to be arrested, but I'd rather be caught than dead. I'm in the middle of the road and don't have time to jump out of the way.

One car screeches to a halt and a door flies open. A police officer leaps out, wearing a hazmat suit. He aims a gun at me. "Don't move!"

I put my hands up. "Don't shoot. I'm just a kid."

"Whatever you are, you're under arrest." The man grabs me by the front of my shirt and slams me much too hard on the bonnet of the car.

I wait for the inevitable click of the handcuffs, but he pauses, distracted. There's the growl of motorbike engines and I glance around to see what's happening. The bikers have turned back and are heading towards us. They brake a short distance away, forming a circle.

There are more bikes than before. Their headlights are on full-beam so we can't see clearly, but I can make out sports bikes and mopeds as well as the more traditional bikes our guys ride. The police are surrounded.

One of the braver police officers uses the built-in loudspeaker in his police car. "You're all in contravention of lockdown regulations. You will surrender for questioning and quarantine."

Silence.

Then laughter.

The jeers get louder, and are followed by howling and whooping and all kinds of other crazy noises. The bikers rev their engines and inch forwards. They outnumber the police at least five to one.

Del jumps off his bike and strides forward, his trusty shotgun in his hand. "I make the rules 'ere, so 'ow abouts yer give me the boy, and ya get lost! Or we'll give yer a whippin' you'll wanna tell yer grandkids about. If you live that long."

The police officer makes one last effort to assert his authority. "It is an offence to threaten a-" he starts over the loudspeaker, but his warning is cut off as a leather-clad biker jumps on top of the car and smashes the speaker with a crowbar, denting the car roof.

Del takes a step towards the officer who's still gripping me by the arm. "Let him go or I'll blow yer legs off."

The officer can see he's outnumbered, but he's loathe to give in. "That's a shotgun, not a pistol. If you shoot me, you'll hit the kid as well."

The guy is so focused on Del and his shotgun that he isn't paying attention to me. It's now or never.

Using all the force I can muster, I step up on the car tyre and push back with my legs. My bike helmet smacks the officer hard in the face, knocking him off-balance. We both tumble to the floor, and I scramble free, running to Del's side.

"Now, hows abouts ya get in yer car, pretty boy," orders Del, waving the shotgun.

Not surprisingly, now he has no leverage, the police officer does as he's told.

"Shame. Looks like ya got a flat!" Del fires the gun, nearly bursting my eardrums and shredding the front tyre of the car.

"Boys, ya know wha' t' do," says Del, hauling me back towards his precious bike. The bikers descend on the police cars, smashing them to pieces. The police officers are terrified, cowering inside.

Del leans over me. "Zac, I like ya, lad, but if ya' fall off my bike again, I'll run yer over meself. Do ya hear me?"

I nod, feeling stupid. "Sorry."

"Mebbe I should 'ave glued yer in yer seat," he chuckles as he lifts me and dumps me on the back of the bike. He slides his shotgun into a holster before climbing on himself. The engine roars into life and we shoot off down the road.

"Who were all those other guys?" I ask, over the radio.

"Ol' friends," says Del. "Bikers like us stick together."

***

As we leave town and career onto a motorway, the overhead signs spark into life, orange letters appearing from nowhere: "THIS IS THE RIDE OF THE RESISTANCE".

My heart races with excitement, knowing that I'm a part of this. No, I'm the *cause* of this. They're doing this for me.

No pressure, Zac. No pressure.

As we approach, the 'D' flickers and changes to become an 'S'.

THIS IS THE RISE OF THE RESISTANCE.

The Rise of the Resistance. That sounds good. This is what my mum risked her freedom for. This is where the tables turn. This is a new dawn.

The Resistance are fighting back.

I have to succeed, or all of this will be in vain.

We might have won the battle, but we're a long way from winning the war.

It all depends on me.

SEVENTEEN

We arrive in London.

The streets are mayhem. I've never seen anything like it, even before the lockdown. Sports bikes zoom past, pulling wheelies and beeping horns. Dirt bikes weave in and out of alleyways, careering down flights of steps, bunny-hopping on and off the pavement.

"This is mad," I mutter to myself, forgetting the others can hear me.

"They ain't gonna like this," agrees Del. "There'll be hell ta pay tomorra'!"

We take the back roads, keen to avoid unwanted attention, even though it looks like the police have way too much to deal with to worry about us.

Soon, we come to a part of the city that's

strange and empty. It's cloaked in darkness, tall buildings blocking out the moonlight. We slow right down, navigating side streets little bigger than alleyways. I'm glad I'm with Del and his crew; I wouldn't want to find myself here alone. But surely there's nothing to be afraid of?

It turns out there is.

A group of large bikes appears at the end of the lane, their headlights way too bright. Del slows to a crawl and stops in front of them.

"Friends of yours?" I ask, my voice sounding nervous through the radio.

"Quiet," urges Del. "Ain't sure wha' this's about."

"You seem to be lost," calls the leader. "You're trespassing. This is our turf."

"Ain't no need to fight," shouts back Del. "We's jus' passin' thru. Resistance bizness."

"Yeah?" The rider inches forward towards us. "What business is that?"

"It's secret." Del shrugs. "So wiv respect, nuffin to do wiv ya."

"Everything that happens here is my business." The enemy biker pulls out a fierce-looking gun and aims it at us. "Start talking."

Del takes a deep breath. "We 'ave a package ta deliver," he explains. "That's all. Jus' let us past and save yer fight for the blues and twos."

"You country-boys don't tell me what to do," says the leader. "Get off your bikes."

"Fine." Del gives a signal to the others. He gets off his bike, and I slip to the ground behind him.

"They're nice bikes," taunts the gang leader. "We might keep them."

"Yeah? Good luck with that." Del moves quicker than I can believe. In one swift movement, he leans forwards, grabs his shotgun and fires it at the biker, blowing him backwards. Another of the Resistance bikers lets off a second shot which hits the fuel tank of the gang leader's bike and it explodes.

Rough hands grab me from behind and force me to the ground. A heavy man lies on top of me, crushing me into the concrete. It's Leo, one of Del's mates.

"Stay down."

There's more gunfire as enemy bikers shoot in our direction through the smoke. After an initial flurry, everything goes silent.

Leo grips my shoulder. "We run on three, you

hear me?"

I nod.

"1...2...3!" Leo jumps up and hauls me to my feet. I stumble as I'm pushed along the alley, back the way we came. I race around a corner to safety, panting in the darkness. A bike approaches, but I can't make out whether it's friend or foe.

As it gets closer, I'm relieved to see it's Del.

"Get yer backside 'ere, NOW!" he shouts, and I pull myself on to the bike, still shaking.

"Where's everyone else?" I shout, as we speed off into the night.

"They have bizness to finish," says Del, in a hard voice.

He stays on bigger roads as we make our way through the city. The riot that the Resistance has started is getting out of control; it's not just a protest any more. We see windows being smashed, graffiti daubed on walls, angry mobs. Somewhere in the distance, a woman screams.

"We're getting close." Del turns off the highway into a small estate full of new houses; the kind of estate I used to live in. Thankfully, out here in the suburbs, there's no sign of motorbikes or gangs. We stop at the end of a street.

"Acacia Lane," he says. "This is where I leave ya. Yer need to find a hundred an' twelve."

"One hundred and twelve, got it." I confirm, sliding off the bike.

"Good luck, young 'un." Del puts his hand on my shoulder. "Yer gonna need it."

"Here." I take off the helmet and hand it to him. "And Del, thanks for everything."

He gives a biker's salute, then speeds off into the distance. I run under the shadow of a nearby tree, wondering if anyone is watching. Even if someone does report me, I'm guessing the police are too busy with the riots to be worried about a kid out in the street. When I'm sure it's calm, I jog up the road, checking the house numbers.

It doesn't take long to find it. Jamie's house is identical to the others, with a small front garden and an empty driveway. There are no lights on; it appears deserted. I slip through the side gate into the back garden.

The kitchen door has marks where it has been forced, like Jamie said. I take a deep breath and ease it open, knowing that anyone could be inside. I move as silently as I can, checking each room. To my relief, the house is empty.

Once I'm sure of that, I turn on lights and take a proper look around. It reminds me of Kieran's place, where I lived for a while before joining the Resistance. It's been so long since I've been anywhere this normal that it makes me want to cry. I think back to my own home, wondering where my mum and brother are right now.

Stay focused, Zac.

I head upstairs. Jamie's room is tidy. No, scratch that. His room is *unbelievably* tidy. He must be a real neat-freak. There are a couple of signs of teenage life; posters of rock bands on the walls and there's a computer in the corner, but none of the usual mess.

I check the time. Quarter to two. Assuming things run to schedule, I have over an hour before I'm picked up by the Collective. That means I have time to shower and change before they come for me. That's a relief.

I wander through to the bathroom. As I strip off my clothes, I try to remember the last time I took a shower in a clean bathroom in a normal house. It must have been at Kieran's, all those months ago. Being in the Resistance, you get used to missing out.

I take my time, enjoying the steaming hot water, dreaming about what life will be like in Arcadia. Maybe I'll even get my own bathroom there? When I dry myself off, I'm amazed at the softness of the clean towel I find on the rail.

I head back to Jamie's room and take some clothes out of his wardrobe. He's the kind of kid who really cares about his appearance; most of the clothes look brand new.

It's late, but I'm used to being up all night, so I'm not tired. That's good, because I won't be getting sleep any time soon.

Waiting is torture but I still have time to kill. Sadly, there's no games console.

How did Jamie survive without one of those during lockdown?

I turn on the TV and flop onto the sofa. The news is full of the protests, with clips of burning bottles being thrown at police officers and bikes screaming through city streets. Rolling text fills in the blanks: "LOCKDOWN RIOTS: Police forces across the country under attack from roving biker gangs... New measures needed to combat violent protests... Concerns over sudden spike in Vicron-X infection following breach of lockdown regulations..."

The news-reader sounds excited. This is the best story they've had for months. "All over Britain, bikers have come out in force this evening. No-one knows how they managed to co-ordinate this protest. Lockdown has been wearing down the patience of the entire nation, and motorbikes across the country have made themselves seen and heard. In some areas, the protests have remained peaceful. But in many city centres, things are out of control. Riot police and the army have been called in to intervene, and the government have promised severe repercussions on those who are taking part in what it describes as random acts of lawlessness and a clear breach of the current regulations."

The news rolls on, but there's nothing on it that I don't already know. I wonder if the disruption will cause any problems for the Collective, and whether they'd still be able to pick me up.

For a while, I channel-surf, looking for anything decent to watch but I can't settle to anything. I keep glancing at the clock.

I head into the kitchen and hunt around for a

snack. The fridge is empty, save for half a carton of milk which has gone off and a few raw vegetables. A loaf in the bread bin is riddled with mould. The cupboards are equally disappointing. All I can find that's edible is half a box of cereal. I take a few handfuls of cornflakes and eat them dry.

By now, there are only ten minutes to go.

I wonder how the Collective will transport me to Arcadia. Layla showed me where it was on a map. It's way up north, so it'll be a long journey and we'll have to get past a lot of checkpoints. Surely, they can't be planning to hack into them all?

I turn off the lights and head outside. The garden is still and quiet. I lean against the wall.

It must be three o'clock by now.

There's a helicopter overhead. At first, I guess it's the police trying to keep track of the protestors, but I realise it's getting closer. It's not a helicopter; it's a drone. A massive one. I stand frozen to the spot as it descends on to the lawn.

The drone is X-shaped with five rotor blades, one at the end of each arm and one in the centre. Underneath them is a small, open-sided cockpit shaped like a bubble with an empty seat. Whoever is flying this thing is doing it by remote.

No-one appears and there are no instructions, but I don't need to be told that this is my ride. I jog forwards and strap myself in.

The drone lifts off and seconds later I'm flying over the dark streets of London. The wind whips around my ears through the open sides of the cockpit and I huddle into Jamie's thick hoodie for warmth. There are no controls in front of me; all I can do is allow myself to be taken wherever the drone wants to go.

I'm now in the hands of the Collective.

And there's no way back.

EIGHTEEN

I shiver and hug myself, surprised at how cold it is in the cockpit.

It's hard to make much out in the darkness, but I can smell the salt air. There's no doubt about it: I'm heading out to sea.

I'm not great at geography, but even I know that means I'm heading east rather than north. Why aren't they taking me to Arcadia? Is this some sort of trap?

If it is, then I'm screwed. I can't jump from this height. Even if I survive the fall, I'm already too far out to swim back to shore. The drone flies lower, closer to the dark waves, a vast expanse of blackness above and below. It feels like it'll go on forever.

I see lights in the far distance. It takes a while

to figure out where they're coming from, but as I draw closer, I can make out a small yacht. The drone flies towards it. It appears that's our destination. Sure enough, we start to descend. There's a gentle bump as it makes contact with the deck.

I unclip the belt and stumble out, my legs wobbly and uncertain as the smooth motion of the drone is replaced by the heave of the waves below.

The ship may not be huge, but it's expensive. It oozes money and class. The drone takes up most of the deck, but there's still room for a luxurious seating area which looks like they designed it for rich business people to entertain their clients.

My stomach heaves and I grab the railing. Seconds later, I throw up over the side. The churning sea below only makes it worse, and I spend a few miserable minutes coughing and retching.

"Feeling sea-sick?" asks a woman, and I spin around. A young couple are emerging from the cabin. They look rich and beautiful, like models in a catalogue.

"Sorry. I've never been out on a boat like this before." I cough again, spitting bile into the ocean below.

"Don't worry. You'll soon adjust." The woman puts her hand on my back. "My name's Cassandra, and this is Anton. We're friends of your uncle."

"We're here to take you to him, to a place called Arcadia."

I'm about to tell him that I already know that, but, just in time, I switch into role. I'm Jamie, a clueless teenager, not Zac, the Resistance spy. "Arcadia?" I ask, as if hearing it for the first time.

"It's amazing. You'll love it there."

"I'll take your word for it." I turn away and retch some more.

"I'll get you some water," says Cassandra, and disappears into the hatch at the front of the boat, next to the cockpit.

"I wasn't expecting this," I admit. "I was told my uncle lived in the UK."

Anton nods. "He does. But right now, travelling across land is difficult. There are checkpoints on all the main roads. It's easier to travel by sea and air. You're much less likely to run into trouble."

"Makes sense."

Cassandra reappears with a bottle. I press it to my lips. Cold water soothes my throat and cleans the worst of the sick from my mouth.

"Thanks," I gasp.

"You don't need to worry about anything from now on," Cassandra reassures me. "Your life is about to change for the better. Arcadia is paradise. You don't know how lucky you are to have an uncle like yours."

"Good to know." I take another swig of the water. "How long will it take to get there?"

"One or two days," says Anton. "Depends a little on the weather. And we need to keep away from the coastline as much as we can."

That's not what I want to hear. I wonder if I'm going to spend all that time feeling sick.

Cassandra can see that I'm worried. "You'll get used to the motion soon, I promise." I hope she's right. We stand there a little longer until we're sure I have nothing left to throw up.

"You must be tired," says Anton. "Let's get you to your cabin."

They lead me through a small door, down to

the cabin below. There's a seating area and galley kitchen. Beyond that is a tiny corridor with several doors.

"There's a small bathroom here," points out Cassandra. Small is an understatement. It's tiny. "And you'll be sleeping in here." The bedroom isn't much bigger. It has nothing but a thin bunk bed and a porthole for a window. I hold on to the wall and breathe deeply, trying to get my stomach to settle.

"I'll get you a bucket," says Anton. "But once you're lying down, you'll feel a lot better."

I'm happy to try anything. I collapse onto the bottom bunk.

"Try to get some sleep," says Cassandra. "We'll chat more tomorrow."

"Ok, thanks."

Once Anton has fetched me a bucket, they close the door, leaving me alone.

The mattress is hard and uncomfortable, but it's no worse than conditions at the pub. Now I'm horizontal, I don't feel so queasy. Hopefully, I'll get used to the motion of the boat. If not, it's going to be a grim few days.

Suck it up, Zac.

There's no point focusing on the negative.

I'm here. I made it. Anton and Cassandra seem nice and they don't seem to have a clue that I'm not Jamie. The plan is on track and I'm heading to Arcadia.

Even if the boat journey is miserable, it's only for a day or two.

It's going to be worth it in the end.

***

I drift in and out of sleep, anxiety creeping into my dreams.

When I wake up, I'm groggy, and it takes me a few moments to work out where I am.

Sunlight streams through the small porthole, making the tiny cabin a little too warm. I can taste bile in my throat. Last night, I took off my hoodie and trainers but slept in the rest of my clothes, being too sick and self-conscious to change. I climb out of the bottom bunk and try to stand up. The motion isn't as bad as I'm expecting. It could be that I'm already getting used to it or maybe the sea isn't as rough as it was last night. Either way, I'm not complaining.

I step into the small bathroom where I use the toilet. I don't expect Anton and Cassandra will be keen to share their toothbrushes, so I put a large dollop of toothpaste on my finger and rub it around my mouth and tongue, substituting the aftertaste of vomit for the minty fresh flavour.

After that, I feel much better. I wash my face, run my fingers through my hair, and make my way outside. I'm almost blinded by the bright sunlight. Shielding my face with my hand, I can see Cassandra and Anton lounging in the seats at the back of the deck.

She's stretched out, a bright red cocktail in her hand. He sits next to her, sipping a beer.

"Jamie!" She calls me over.

"Hey," I smile and stumble over to them. There's less wind today, only a gentle breeze. The boat is much more steady, but still takes some getting used to.

"How are you?" Cassandra puts down her drink and takes off her sunglasses, looking me up and down.

"Not too bad. A lot better than last night."

"That's good. Take a seat."

I slump down, taking in the view. Blue sky

with a few wispy clouds. Sparkling blue ocean. "This is amazing. I've never been out at sea before, not like this."

"It's quite something, isn't it!" Anton leans down and pulls a bottle of water out of a small mini-fridge. He throws it to me. "Keep drinking. You need to get your fluids back."

I nod and twist the cap off the bottle. As soon as I gulp it, my stomach makes a loud gurgling noise, making Cassandra laugh.

"Are you hungry?" she asks.

I feel myself going red. "I guess. I don't think there's anything left in my stomach."

"I'll get you something." Cassandra disappears, leaving Anton and me alone.

"Who's driving?" I ask.

"No-one," explains Anton. "It's just us three on board. But I set the controls to auto-pilot. I check on them every now and again to make sure we're on course and there aren't any unexpected problems."

"Is it your boat?"

"It was," he says. "Now it belongs to the Collective."

"The Collective?" I pretend it's the first time

I've heard the term.

"It's something your uncle set up. It's like an organisation. Well, more like a movement that people join. We live with one another, in Arcadia."

"All in the same place? That sounds hectic."

"We have our own houses and stuff. On the same site." Anton leans back in his seat, staring out to sea. "But Arcadia is more than a place. It's a vision of the future. It's how things need to be."

I ask a question that's been bugging me. "Does everyone have to stay inside there? Is it locked down?"

Anton laughs. "No, we don't need to stay indoors. No-one worries about the virus."

"How come? Do you all get temp-shots?"

"We have a vaccine. Once you have it, you can't catch Vicron-X. You're safe for life."

Then, the rumours are true. Layla wasn't making it up. A vaccine exists and the Collective are keeping it from the rest of us.

"You serious? How come you don't share this vaccine with everyone else?"

"It's not that simple," sighs Anton. "You'll learn all about it when we get there. Your tutors will soon get you caught up."

"Tutors?" The idea that I might have to do lessons comes as a surprise. I guess I thought that living in a virtual paradise would be more like a holiday. "There's a school?"

"Afraid so." Anton grins. "Our version of one, anyway."

Cassandra returns with some hot buttered toast. I tear into it, glad to have something that won't unsettle my stomach.

"Looks like you needed that," she observes.

"I did," I mumble, my mouth full.

"Jamie's just found out he's going to have learn stuff in Arcadia," says Anton. "I don't think he's looking forward to going back to school."

Cassandra smiles. "Don't worry. It's different to the kind of school that you're used to. Trust me, you'll enjoy it."

I nod. There might be some advantages. It might provide easy access to some computers for a start. "So, what's the plan for today?"

"I'm afraid there's not a lot to do around here. When you're out at sea, you just have to get used to talking and relaxing and enjoying the scenery." Anton racks his brains. "When you've finished your breakfast, I can show you the controls if you like?"

"I'm sure he doesn't want you to bore him with those," says Cassandra.

"No, it sounds cool," I say. I'd like to see how the boat works. It might be useful.

Anton smiles at his partner. "I knew he'd be interested."

"He's probably just humouring you," suggests Cassandra. "Don't let him drone on for too long, Jamie. There are some books in the cabin below if you get desperate."

"I might check them out later. Thanks."

Sitting there in the bright sunshine and cool breeze, looking at the clear sky and brilliant blue water, I can cope with a couple of boring days. If everyone in the Collective is as friendly as Anton and Cassandra, then I have nothing to be afraid of.

And I can't wait to see what Arcadia's like.

NINETEEN

We spend the day relaxing. I keep asking questions about Arcadia, which they do their best to answer.

"You'll have to wait and see," says Cassandra, for what must be the fifth time. "But you won't be disappointed, I promise."

We also chat about other things. They ask me what it was like growing up before and after the lockdown. I have to keep reminding myself to answer as Jamie, not as Zac, but I don't say anything that will give the game away. I realise that if I'm going to keep up the pretence, then I have to stop pretending to be Jamie. I have to actually *be* Jamie, to convince myself that's who I am, and believe the things I say. That might sound nuts, but the more I do it, the easier it gets.

True to his word, Anton shows me the cockpit. The impressive-looking onboard computer is so simple that almost anyone can operate it. "All you have to do is use the satellite navigation to pinpoint your destination, and it will calculate the safest route," he says, pointing at the screen. "We can also add in the variable that we want to stay a specific distance from the shore."

"And then you toggle the auto-pilot on?" I ask, fascinated.

"Yep, simple as that."

"What about when you're not on auto-pilot? How do you steer the boat? Do you just turn the wheel?"

"Pretty much." Anton shows me the other controls. "This increases and decreases the thrust, so you can go faster or slower. And you can reverse the thrust to slow down—that's like braking on the water."

"And what are these controls for?" I point to another console on the side. That one looks portable, as if you can pick it up and carry it around.

"Oh, that's nothing to do with the ship. That's the controller for the drone. Similar idea though.

You use the Sat-Nav system to input your target and choose your altitude and any via points on the way." He shows me how to add a destination.

"The drone is faster than the boat, right?" I ask, interested.

"Much faster."

"So how come you didn't use the drone to get me all the way to Arcadia? Wouldn't that have been easier?"

"It's too far," explains Anton. "The drone has a range of about forty miles. And it needs recharging after a long flight. It's still charging now. We'll use it to drop you off at Arcadia as soon as we get close enough. It should have a full battery by then."

***

The rest of the day, I lounge about on the deck, eat some healthy vegetable wraps, and chill with Anton and Cassandra. It's nice to relax for a change, away from all the stress of lockdown and the Resistance.

The sun is getting lower in the sky when a loud beeping noise cuts through the quiet. Anton jumps up and heads for the cockpit.

"What is it?" I ask.

Cassandra squints at the horizon. "Proximity alarm. Another ship must be nearby. Anton will try to take us around them."

A few minutes pass, then we hear our engine stop and the boat slows down.

Anton returns, looking stressed. "We've got trouble. A Quarantine Agency vessel is heading towards us. They've announced their intention to board."

"Can't we outrun them?" I realise it's a stupid question as soon as I say it.

"Their ship is much more powerful. And they've jammed our communications, so I can't even inform the Collective."

"What do we do?" Cassandra sounds panicked.

"There's nothing we can do but wait for them. Except, we could try to keep Jamie safe."

Cassandra glances out to sea. "We don't have long."

"Come over here." Anton pulls me into the shadow of the cockpit, out of view of the approaching vessel. "They won't know how many of us are on board. If we hide you, you might be able to escape later."

"He could hide in one of the storage containers?" suggests Cassandra.

"They might check. We should throw him over the side."

"Wait, what?" My voice sounds weak and pathetic. "I can't swim to the shore from here! It's miles away!"

Anton looks frustrated. "I mean we could drop you into the water on a long rope. If they arrest us, as soon as the Quarantine Agency have left, you can pull yourself back on board and stay hidden. With any luck, they'll stop jamming our comms once they've got us in custody, so you could message your uncle and let him know what's happened."

I glance nervously at the water. "Sounds like a long shot."

"It is, but if you don't try it, we'll all be in quarantine. And if we can't get a message to the Collective, they won't come to rescue us."

"It's worth a try," I concede. "What do I do?"

"Whatever it is, you need to hurry," says Cassandra, standing at the railing. "They're getting closer."

Anton grabs some rope. He ties it around my waist and between my legs, making a kind of harness. "I'm afraid it's not going to be comfortable, but it's the best I can do."

"It'll be fine," I reassure him, sounding much braver than I feel.

He ties the other end of the rope to the deck railing and pulls a heavy storage container in front of it. "Good luck Jamie. I hope we meet again in Arcadia."

"Me too."

"Over you go." Anton pushes me gently towards the railing and I climb over. The drop is a lot further than I expect.

"Don't sit there. Climb down the rope."

I glance down, hesitating "It's too far. I don't think I can."

"Fine. I'll lower you," says Anton.

Taking the slack, he starts to ease me down the side. I cling to the rope for dear life as I descend towards the water. The harness tightens around my jeans.

"How are you doing?" calls Anton, his voice little more than a whisper.

"I'm ok." The engine of the approaching boat is getting loud now.

"I have to let go."

The words are barely out his mouth before I drop like a stone, plunging into the water. It's like being dropped in a bucket of ice. There's a sudden jerk and a burning sensation near my groin as the rope digs in, tightening around my legs. I splash about, gasping for breath. The rope is just long enough to keep my head above the surface, waves lapping against my nose and mouth.

I stay as quiet as I can, my teeth chattering, making it hard to hear what's happening on the boat above. Over the constant lapping of the waves, I can make out Anton's indignant voice: "... just me and my girlfriend. We're nothing to do with the Resistance!"

The man he's talking to doesn't sound convinced. "And you happen to be out here the day after the largest uprising the country has ever seen?"

"We're out here sailing," cuts in Cassandra. "We didn't even know about any protests."

"Sailing is breaking the law unless you have a

legitimate reason. Why are you out of your homes?"

"We needed to get away. We were desperate for a holiday." Cassandra is trying to soothe it over, but her charm is wasted on the Quarantine Agency.

"Is there anyone else on board?"

"No. Just us."

"Search the vessel and have these two taken into quarantine."

"We don't need to be quarantined," argues Anton. "We haven't seen anyone. We're clear of the virus."

"All breaches of lockdown result in immediate quarantine, followed by further charges. Those are the rules."

There are some last pleas from Cassandra and Anton and some clattering around on the deck, before the officer speaks again. "You three, search the ship. Check there's no-one else here."

"Yes, sir."

After that, everything goes quiet.

The sun has set, and the sky is getting darker.

I bob up and down in the water. My hands are too numb to grip the rope properly and I'm not sure how much longer I can float here in the freezing water. After a while, part of me *wants* to be found, just so I can get warm and dry.

But I need to stay hidden.

Hang in there, Zac.

There's not a lot else I can do.

TWENTY

I've almost given up hope when I hear a voice on the deck. "The vessel's clear, sir. There's no-one else on board."

"Good. Secure the tow-rope and return to the main ship."

I swear under my breath. I'd been hoping that once they finished their search, they'd sail off, leaving the yacht behind. I had fantasies of piloting the boat to Arcadia, programming the navigation system that Anton had showed me how to use. But, of course, they wouldn't leave an empty boat at sea. They're taking it with them.

The engine on the larger ship starts up and, with a sudden jerk, our yacht also begins to move. The rope tugs me forward, coughing and spluttering as my body is dragged along in the water. Within seconds, I've lost both my trainers. I'm lucky that my jeans and underwear are held in place by the rope or I'd lose those as well.

I cling on, salt water surging around my face and body, finding its way into my nose and mouth. I push past the exhaustion and try to pull my tired and numb body out of the slipstream. Once my head is clear of the waves, I retch and vomit out seawater.

The large ship's engine is loud enough to drown out my pathetic noises, but I try to keep my panting and gasping to a minimum as I climb further. My hands are slippery from the water and my limbs scream at me to stop. I ignore them and press on, one hand over the other, inching up the rope, the water rushing below.

There's barely any daylight left. That means I'm less likely to be seen. But it also means it's getting colder.

Keep going, Zac.

I force myself upwards. I wish I hadn't lost my trainers in the water. They'd have provided a better grip than my soggy-socked feet, which are already sore and keep slipping.

By sheer grit and determination, I somehow

get a grip on the ship's railing. With one last burst of energy, I drag myself up and over, before collapsing on the deck, gasping for breath and rubbing my hands.

I glance around, worried that someone has seen or heard me, but the deck is quiet and empty. The cockpit hides me from anyone on the larger Quarantine Agency ship.

I tug the rope harness off my legs, feeling a sense of relief.

The climb has helped to warm me up, but I'm still shivering and there's no time to spare. I need to contact the Collective.

It's dark in the cockpit. I can just about make out the controls from the glow of the screens, and I sit in front of them. Switching the comms unit on is easy, but a message flashes up: "Error. No Signal."

I groan. It's useless. Either the yacht is too far from shore or the Quarantine Agency are still blocking the signal.

What now?

Anton suggested I might stay hidden on the boat until we docked, then sneak ashore. But that's not a great plan. Wherever we land, I bet there'll be loads of security.

Glancing around, I get a better idea. The drone! It's been charging since I travelled on it the previous night. Surely, it could get me to shore? I grab the controller from the side and check our location. We're only ten miles from land, and Anton had said the drone could cover four times that distance when fully charged.

It's my best shot. As soon as I make it to the coast, I'll hunt out a computer and contact the Collective. They can send someone to rescue me and also arrange for Anton and Cassandra to be released.

I pore over the map, plotting where I want the drone to land. I choose a spot near to a small village. There's not likely to be much of a police presence in a place like that, but there should be computers.

I climb down to the deck, taking the portable controller with me. It's tempting to hunt around in the cabin, to see if I can find some dry clothes, but it's too risky. The longer I stay on the yacht, the more likely I am to get caught. It's now or never.

I climb into the drone. A small pool of

seawater oozes onto the soft leather of the seat.

As soon as I press the 'Launch' button, the rotors will start turning and that's bound to attract attention. I don't know how long the drone takes to warm up, before it's ready to lift off, but it's a risk I have to take.

Here goes nothing.

I stab the button. A quiet hum fills the air, which becomes more of a buzz as the blades spin faster.

There's a shout from the main ship. I've been spotted.

"Come on, come on!" There's no way to hurry this up and the officers will board any moment now.

There's a jerk as the drone takes off and swoops forward. Several Quarantine Agency officers are gathered on the deck of the larger ship, pointing and shouting. They duck as we fly overhead, and I can't resist giving them a small wave.

Seconds later, I'm zooming over the water towards the shore, the boats miles behind.

I've done it. I've escaped.

I might still make it to Arcadia.

It's good that I can hold on to hope, because I'm going to land in the middle of nowhere in the darkness, still soaked to the skin. And I don't have any shoes.

I might have escaped the Quarantine Agency, but I've simply exchanged one set of problems for another.

My ordeal is far from over.

And I still have a long way to go.

TWENTY-ONE

Nothing in my life goes to plan.

A warning appears on the console: "LOW CHARGE. EMERGENCY LANDING WILL BEGIN SHORTLY."

According to the display, I'm close to the shore, but I'm already losing altitude as the drone prepares to touch down. I glance out the cockpit to see waves a few metres below. Looks like I'm about to get drenched for the second time today.

But there's hope; lights on the horizon. Maybe the drone will hold out long enough to get me to dry land. If not, at least it won't be too far to swim.

Numbers appear on the screen. A countdown. "EMERGENCY LANDING IN 5... 4... 3..."

I can feel the spray on my face as we hurtle towards the shore.

"2... 1..."

I expect to be plunged into freezing water as I drop the last few metres, but instead of a splash there's a dull squelch. The drone is still, its rotors slowing. It looks like I've landed on a beach and I step out. Wet mud sucks at my feet. Mud-flats. Just perfect. I abandon the drone and trudge towards solid ground.

Every step is difficult in the stinking sludge. It reminds me of the muddy trail I ran with Kieran on one of our last missions. I wonder what he's up to now, and how he, Trix and the real Jamie are getting on. They think I'm living in luxury. Instead, I'm cold, wet and knee-deep in mud.

A deep puddle makes me lose my balance, my leg sinking to the thigh and sending me sprawling forwards. I pull back, dragging my leg out. I need to be careful. If I get sucked too deep, I could die out here, drowning in the muck. What a way to go.

I push on. The shore doesn't seem any closer and I'm losing the will to live. The only thing that keeps me going is the fact that I literally can't stop. Whenever I stand still, my feet get sucked further down. There's nowhere to sit and no way to rest. Mud splatters my face and body as I tug my legs up and out, again and again, my body aching with the effort.

I have to make it to Arcadia and complete my mission. Everything depends on it. I know that. We have to stop the Collective. They have a vaccine and they're keeping everyone else in lockdown. Anton and Cassandra admitted as much.

But then, they also seemed to be such nice people. They didn't appear to be evil. They did everything they could to save me. How could they be part of a selfish plot? It doesn't make sense.

I can't dwell on that. Right now, I just have to get to safety.

A few more steps. The mud here doesn't seem so deep, only reaching my ankles. A short distance away, I can see sand dunes. That gives me one last burst of energy. Before long, I'm limping across sharp stones.

I reach the dunes and collapse, panting.

I want to stay here; I need to rest. But I'm also shivering, and in danger of getting hypothermia.

After only a few minutes, I drag myself to my feet and force myself to carry on, breaking into a gentle jog as I head further inland.

***

Past the dunes is a small road. It has to lead somewhere, and there's no sign of traffic. I run down it, more hopeful as my feet pound the hard, smooth tarmac. In the distance, I see lights.

As I get closer, I realise it's a farm. A barn and several small outbuildings cluster around a large house and yard. Lights are on in the main house, but the other buildings are cloaked in darkness.

I come to the barn first, relieved to find the door isn't locked. I peer inside but there's very little to see; just a huge mound of hay piled up from floor to ceiling. That's not much use to me. I need to find a computer, but I'm beginning to have doubts that I'll find anything more high-tech than a tractor in a place like this.

I creep through the farmyard, my feet sliding in stuff I don't even want to think about. Light spills out from one of the farmhouse windows. No-one has drawn the curtains, so I can easily see in. There's nothing of interest, just an empty lounge with old floral sofas and a large fireplace.

Don't get me wrong: it looks warm and cosy, and I'd love to curl up and sleep somewhere like that. But that's not going to happen. I feel like a poor, hungry kid with his face pressed against a sweet shop window, eyeing up stuff he can never have.

They've left the porch open at the back, and I can see a few pairs of wellies inside. That's a start. I need something for my feet.

When I try them on, though, I discover that they're way too big. Every time I take a step, my foot comes out. It's no use. I wonder whether I dare try the back door, but as I'm about to turn the handle, I hear a dog bark.

I turn and run, dashing to the hay-barn and pushing the door shut. Hopefully, no-one has seen me and they won't let the dog out.

I fumble around in the darkness, climbing the mountain of hay. There's a gap between two bales and I collapse into it. My clothes are damp and uncomfortable so I strip down to my underwear.

Now, I feel a lot better. Even though I'm naked

and the night air is cool, I no longer have the damp fabric against my skin. I snuggle down in the hay. It's hardly comfortable, but at least I stop shivering.

I'm not planning on staying here for long, just for a quick rest. Then I'll push on and find some other houses, ones without dogs and with access to the Net.

But, I'm exhausted. I've fought the waves, climbed a rope and trudged through knee-deep muck. My eyes are getting heavy.

Come on, Zac, get moving.

I want to, but I can't.

I don't have the energy to do anything else tonight.

Except sleep.

TWENTY-TWO

I awake with a start.

It's still dark in the barn, but I've slept for hours. Morning can't be far off.

I grimace as I pull on my damp t-shirt, hoodie and the still-wet jeans. Once I'm dressed, I slide down the haystack and ease open the barn door, peering out to the dark and silent farmyard. It's lucky I didn't sleep any longer: if I'd woken when it was light, I'd have had to spend the whole day hiding away in the barn. There's a good chance I'd have been caught.

I slip outside and sprint down the farm track. Once I'm back on the road, I slow to a jog as I make my way further along the coast. If I plotted the route correctly when I programmed the drone, the village can't be far away.

I make a list in my head of what I need to do. Find some dry clothes and shoes. Contact the Collective. Eat something.

The sky has gone from black to dark blue and I can make out the dark shapes of houses on the horizon. Dawn will soon be here, and people will wake, but I don't have much further to go.

***

I'm nearly there.

That's what I think only seconds before I hear vehicles approaching.

Hide!

To my left, a wooden gate leads into a large crop-field. I climb over and slip behind a hedge.

The vehicles slow down and come to a stop. I catch a glimpse of a logo through the branches. Quarantine Agency vans. Agents are climbing out, pulling on infra-red visors. If they're using those, there's no point staying here; my body heat will give me away.

Fortunately, they're also wearing full protective clothing, dressed up like astronauts. They won't be able to move very fast, so my best bet is to run. I dash to the other end of the field, stumbling over the freshly ploughed dirt.

As I glance back, I see two agents climbing over the gate, bright head-torches shining towards me like floodlights. They've seen me and they're giving chase.

The fence at the edge of the field is topped with rusty barbed wire. I scramble over it, scratching my legs and tearing a hole in my jeans. Dropping down the other side, I keep on running. I look back to see the officers are struggling with the fence, worried that they'll rip their protective suits. That buys me some time. I sprint past cows, their eyes glinting in the darkness, creeping me out. I'm almost out of breath. I can't keep up this pace for long.

There's a strange sound in the air, like a snap followed by a whoosh-whoosh of spinning rope. Something wraps itself around my legs, binding my ankles together and sending me tumbling forward. I land in a big pile of cow muck.

I roll over and sit up, trying to remove the cable that's tied around my feet, but the agents aren't far away. By the time I get the cord untangled, they're close enough to grab hold.

One of them lifts me off the ground.

"Let me go!" It's pointless squirming, but the adrenaline takes over. I bite down hard on the officer's arm and he yells in pain. He loosens his grip just enough for me to turn and kick him hard in the groin. He doubles over, finally letting go.

I turn to run but his partner dives at my legs, taking me back down into the mud. He kneels on my back.

"It's over, lad. We've got you." He says it with satisfaction.

Cold metal handcuffs click around my wrists, tight enough to hurt, and I'm hauled to my feet. I want to wipe the cow muck off my face but can't. I try to rub it off on my shoulder.

The wounded officer stands up. I can see how angry he is through his visor.

"The little punk has compromised my suit."

His colleague pushes me ahead of him. "They'll make you do quarantine again."

That isn't what the man wants to hear. He turns to me, hatred on his face. "You're gonna pay for that."

"What do you mean?" I blurt out, worried.

"Quarantine is bad enough at the best of

times. But we have ways of making it worse for troublemakers like you."

They drag me to the van.

"So, this is the brat who kept us up all night?" asks the driver, who's been waiting in the road.

"Yep, and he bit Spencer. Made his arm bleed."

"Filthy animal," spat the man. "Look at the state of him."

I must appear pretty pathetic: shivering in the chilly breeze, wearing torn clothes and covered in muck.

I don't say anything as I'm pushed into the back. I'm forced down on the floor with my hands still cuffed behind me as the vehicle moves off.

All my efforts to escape capture have achieved nothing, other than causing me a lot of pain and stress. Now I have no hope of contacting the Collective.

I always knew the chances of succeeding in my mission were small, but I figured I'd at least make it to Arcadia.

I've failed to even do that.

Instead of five-star luxury, I'm about to face the horrors of quarantine.

And the Resistance won't even know I've failed.

TWENTY-THREE

The journey is rough.

I'm sure the driver is swerving around corners way too fast, just so I get thrown around in the back.

My fear grows with every passing minute. What are they going to do to me? Surely, it can't be *that* bad. As a government organisation, the Quarantine Agency can't torture me or anything. It won't be like my time with the criminal gang; there will be rules they have to follow. But no-one seems to care that I'm sliding about, my hands cuffed behind me, or that I keep crashing into the metal panels.

Finally, the van stops.

We're here, wherever here is.

The men open the doors, looking like robots in

their grey coveralls and visors.

"Out." One man grabs my hoodie and pulls me to my feet, dragging me out. I stumble as I hit the tarmac.

"Hey, careful," I complain.

"You bit one of our officers." He shoves me forward. The message is clear: *Get used to it.*

The huge building in front of us looks like a white box that's been left in the middle of nowhere. There's nothing but open fields for miles around. A neat blue sign identifies it as the "East Anglia Quarantine Centre". I've seen scarier places, but there's something about it that sends a shiver down my spine.

I'm pushed through a small door into a changing room, not that different to the ones at my old school. The walls are tiled and there are a few wooden benches. Against the back wall are showers with no curtains or cubicles. Clearly, privacy isn't a big deal here.

The man's grip tightens on my hoodie, almost strangling me. "I'm going to take off the cuffs and you're going to get out of those stinking clothes and take a shower. You understand?"

"Yeah, sure. No problem." I don't have any

complaints about that. I'm desperate to get clean. I've been smelling nothing but cow muck since they caught me.

He looks me in the eye. "I should warn you: if you try anything then we'll do this the hard way, and you do not want that to happen."

I gulp and nod. I don't know what that means but I have no intention of finding out.

As soon as the cuffs are off, I rub my sore wrists.

The man steps back towards the wall, standing next to his colleague. "Now, strip," he orders.

"Aren't you gonna leave?"

"Nope." The man smiles behind his visor, as if I've said something amusing.

Suck it up, Zac.

I pull off my clothes, right down to my underwear. "You want me to take these off as well?"

"Now you're getting it."

I turn away and pull off the grubby trunks. One of the men presses a button and water cascades down in front of me. I test it with my hand, shocked to find it's freezing. I hold back.

The man calls over. "What are you waiting

for?"

"For it to warm up."

There's a hollow laugh. "We save the *hot* water for people who follow the rules. Now, get in there and get clean."

I edge forwards and force myself under the cold water, letting it wash through my filthy hair and down my body. My teeth are chattering, but it's good to watch the muck get washed away. After a minute or two, I glance up at the two men.

"Any chance of some shower gel?" I ask.

That annoys them and they turn off the water. I stand, dripping wet, on the tiled floor. One of them throws me a thin towel. I dry myself as quick as I can while they dump some clothes on the floor.

"Get dressed."

"Thanks." I say, cheerfully. I want to let them know that their tough-guy act doesn't scare me.

Even though it does.

The clothes are prison-wear: a white vest, old-fashioned underwear, grey socks and an orange boiler suit which covers my whole body and buttons up at the front. It's way too big. I have to turn up the bottom of the trouser legs so they don't trip me up. There are some black plimsolls so I at least have something to protect my feet.

"What now?"

"Now we take you for processing. Hands behind your back."

"Is that necessary?" I ask, as he pulls out the handcuffs.

"Nope." He secures them around my wrist, smirking as if he's said something funny.

***

I'm pushed into a tiny room. All it contains is a metal chair.

"Sit," orders the officer, and I do as I'm told. He slams the door, leaving me alone.

There's a blank screen on the wall. After a few seconds, an image appears. The head and shoulders of a fierce-looking grey-haired woman in her fifties. She reminds me of the headteacher at my school.

"Welcome to the East Anglia Quarantine Centre." Her tone makes it clear that I'm anything but welcome. "What's your name?"

I freeze. I haven't thought this through and I

don't know what to say. If I tell them I'm Zac McAllister, then they'll soon discover I'm a runaway, and that I'm wanted by the police. They might even link me to the Resistance. Who knows how long they'll lock me up for? But if I use Jamie's name, that might be a problem too. They might have Jamie's photograph or fingerprints or DNA on file and they'll find out I'm lying.

I guess I could make something up, but I've already taken too long to answer. So, I stay silent, figuring that's the least risky course of action.

The woman narrows her eyes. "No name, huh? Well, if that's how you want to play it... I don't suppose you're going to tell me your date of birth either?"

I look away.

"I'll have to guess, then. Let's see, you must be nineteen. That will allow us to process you as an adult. None of those extra privileges that kids get."

"But I'm only thirteen," I object.

"Oh, it speaks," she says, sarcasm dripping from her voice. She leans back and looks at me. "You escaped from the Quarantine Agency ship when we arrested your parents. We know they have links to the Resistance. If you answer all of my questions, I'll process you as a child and arrange for you to have an easy stay here. But if you lie to me or hold things back, then you'll regret it. Understand?"

I force myself to stay calm. She doesn't know a lot if she believes Anton and Cassandra are my parents. "Whatever."

"Where were you all heading in the boat? And where had you come from?"

"We're not part of the Resistance," I say. "You've got it all wrong."

She sighs as if she has better things to do than interrogate me. "You might think your parents are the good guys, but the Resistance is putting everyone in danger and they need to be stopped. You can help us do that. You were out at sea on the same day as the worst lockdown protests our country has ever seen with an advanced drone on board. We want to know what your parents were doing, and which Resistance cell they're part of."

"I don't know anything about the Resistance."

"You're lying. And until you're willing to share that information, your life is going to be pretty miserable."

I shrug and stay silent.

"So, you won't answer any of my questions?"

I give her a defiant stare, trying to act like Kieran would if he were here.

"That's a shame. But you'll change your mind in a few days. I'll put you on Grinson's corridor. He'll teach you some manners."

The screen goes blank before I can respond.

At least that means I can't cave.

Not yet, anyway.

TWENTY-FOUR

I'm taken along blank corridors, then down a staircase into the basement. Every so often, we stop at a coded gate at the end of a section. We have to wait for a green light to allow us through.

My heart sinks as we go deeper into the complex. As far as I can tell, breaking out of here is not an option.

We stop outside room 206 and the officers swipe a card. The door clicks open and I'm pushed inside.

Grey. That's all I can see. The walls are grey, the floor is grey, even the ceiling is grey. There's a thin ledge on one wall with a super-thin mattress on top of it, along with a brown folded blanket and a stained pillow. The only other furniture is a desk attached to the wall and a plastic chair. There's a camera in the corner, watching my every move.

An opening leads through to a tiny bathroom with a metal toilet and sink. The toilet doesn't even have a seat. There's no shower cubicle, just a showerhead and a drain in the floor.

"Home, sweet home," jokes the officer.

I want to answer back but I'm too horrified to speak. I can't stay here. There isn't any daylight, just LED strips overhead. The only thing that gives me hope is that one wall has a large screen and a keyboard. With any luck, I can at least watch TV or access the Net. And if I can get on the Net, I can contact the Collective.

"Not so tough now, eh?" The officers leave, slamming the door behind them.

I check the room again, hoping I missed something the first time. I tap on the keyboard but nothing happens; the screen remains blank. Maybe there's a way to switch it on? There's some kind of plastic cover near the floor, but when I lift it, it just reveals a plug point.

I sigh and slump down on the mattress. Turns out it's even less comfortable than it appears.

They designed quarantine to keep you apart

from everyone else. I expected isolation and a certain amount of boredom, but there's literally *nothing* to do. I lie back on the bed, forcing myself not to panic. After all, I'm clean, dry and reasonably safe. I might as well make the most of it.

I close my eyes and try to sleep.

***

"On your feet!" The voice is way too loud.

I open my eyes. A man's face fills the screen in front of me. He looks young, more like a student than a quarantine officer. But he also looks mean. His eyes, nose and mouth are squashed together. Red blotches and spots cover the skin and his dark hair hangs down in greasy clumps. It's not a pleasant face to look at, especially when it's three times bigger than it should be.

"I said: on your feet, 206. Are you deaf?"

I clamber off the bed, rubbing sleep from my eyes.

"My name is Officer Grinson. I'm responsible for you during your stay here."

"Great."

"Oh, trust me. It won't be great. You bit one of my colleagues today. Because of you, they're going to spend two months in quarantine."

I shrug. "If you made quarantine nicer, that wouldn't be a problem."

"Don't worry. He'll be in a much better room than this. He'll have a sofa, a comfortable bed, a nice big window with a view of the countryside. And, like most people in quarantine, he'll get to watch TV and use the Net as much as he wants."

I look around me at the grey walls. "But I don't?"

"We've assigned you to a high-security room. We picked out the worst one we could find. I've also disabled your keyboard so you can't use your screen. And until you're ready to answer some questions, you're going to get *very* bored and uncomfortable."

"Will I at least get *some* screen-time?"

Grinson smiles in a way that makes my stomach turn. "You won't get anything."

"For the whole sixty days?" The cramped room already seems smaller than it did. "I'm just a kid. You can't treat me like this. I have rights."

"Not according to my records, 206. I have you

down as a nineteen-year-old anonymous suspect who has been arrested for clear violations of lockdown, possible Resistance activity and assaulting a Quarantine Agency officer. Given that you also refused to co-operate with our investigation, you barely have the right to breathe. Once you're ready to talk, you might get some privileges. Some of the boys have placed bets on how long you'll last."

"That's not right! That's illegal! You can't do stuff like that!"

"I can do what I like. And I'd be careful if I were you. You need to show me some respect. You wouldn't want to make me mad. That won't end well for you."

"Respect?" I can't believe what I'm hearing. "You're sick."

Grinson examines me like he's working out which part he despises the most. "I'm looking forward to seeing if you're still acting this tough in a few days time."

"Whatever." I sit down on the bed.

"I didn't tell you to sit down."

"Yeah, well I don't take orders from you. What you gonna do? I already have the smallest room in the world and no screen-time. It can't get any worse."

"If you believe that, you're more stupid than I thought."

"I don't care." I lie down and stare at the ceiling, ignoring him.

"Are you hungry, 206?"

That gets my attention. I haven't eaten since I was with Anton and Cassandra. "Yeah. Why?"

"Then you might want to rethink your attitude."

I push myself up on my elbows. "You mean I don't get any food unless I do what you say?"

"That's exactly what I mean."

I shrug as if I'm not concerned. "I'll starve. And you'll get into a load of trouble for letting it happen."

"We'll see."

The screen goes blank.

I'm left lying there in the grey room, my stomach grumbling.

Both Grinson and I know it takes a long time to die from starvation.

And we both know something else; I'll break long before it happens.

It's just a matter of time.

TWENTY-FIVE

I have no idea how long I lie there. There's no way to keep track of time and nothing to distract me from my empty stomach. The more I try not to think about it, the more I do. I'm desperate for food.

I curse myself for being weak and pathetic, but I have to give in. I can't spend another hour like this, let alone another day. I need to swallow my pride.

I walk over to the screen and glance up at the camera, hoping that he can hear me. "Hey, Officer Grinson. You win, ok? I'll follow your orders. I need food."

There's no response.

I wonder if he wants me to beg. "I'll do anything you ask. Please, just feed me."

Still nothing.

I pace around for a bit, frustrated. I bet he'd love to see me punch a wall or get angry. I don't want to give him the satisfaction.

So, I sit on the bed and wait.

***

By the time the screen comes to life, I'm desperate.

Grinson is eating a large cake, stuffing it into his mouth, crumbs and cream going everywhere.

"On your feet, 206."

I jump up and shuffle over to the screen.

He wipes his mouth with his sleeve and holds up what's left of the cake. "This is delicious."

I say what he wants to hear. "Ok, you win."

"What was that?"

"I said, you win." I say it loudly but keep my voice even. I don't want to annoy him. "I'll do whatever you want. I need food."

He takes another large bite and looks at me as he chews and swallows, making me wait. "Let's see, shall we? Stand in the corner, face to the wall."

I turn and shuffle towards it.

"If you want any food, don't move an inch."

"For how long?"

"Until I tell you otherwise. I'll be watching."

If I was bored before, it's even worse now. I can't even move. There has to be a way out of this.

Come on, Zac. Think!

The screen must be connected to the Net. I have to get online. It would only take a matter of minutes to send a message to the Collective. Then, hopefully, they could arrange a rescue.

Perhaps if I do everything Grinson asks, he'll ease up and let me have some screen-time? There must be some way I can persuade him. I wonder whether I should make some stuff up about the Resistance. That might make him think I'm co-operating, but it might also get Anton and Cassandra convicted, which could cause problems with the Collective. I can't risk it. For now, I just have to stand here and see what he asks me to do next.

The thought of food spurs me on. I'm not expecting anything amazing in a place like this, but I'd eat anything right now.

Please don't leave me here for long.

But he does.

Minutes drag into hours.

I have to fight the temptation to give up and crash on to the bed. I need the food too badly. I wonder how often he's going to make me do this.

I can't do it every day. I just can't.

After an age, I hear his voice. "Learnt some manners, 206?"

"Yes, sir."

"Good. You can turn around and face me." He leans back in his chair, his hands behind his head, emphasising his absolute power.

"Can I ask you something? If I'm good, could I earn some screen-time? I need some entertainment in here. At least an hour a day, else I'll go mad."

"Will you tell us about the Resistance?" asks Grinson.

"I don't know anything. But I'll do *anything* else you ask." I feel like I'm selling my soul to the devil.

Grinson narrows his eyes. "I don't need to do any deals with you. I own you. And unless you tell us what we want to know, then you have nothing to look forward to except pain and suffering. Is that clear?"

"But I want…"

"Quiet. It doesn't matter what you want. All that matters is what I want. A few more hours in the corner will help you to understand that."

He disappears, leaving me staring at my reflection in the blank screen. So much for trying to persuade him to give me a reward.

I curse inwardly as I turn and face the corner. The man has me under his control. The days stretch ahead of me like an eternity. I'll never survive sixty days of this. I haven't even lasted the first twenty-four hours and I already want to cry.

Grinson is only just getting started.

And I'm already done.

TWENTY-SIX

Every second, I long for Grinson's face to appear.

Yet that's also what I'm most afraid of.

He's messing with my head.

When he finally shows up, my whole body is tense.

"Well, 206. As you've done as you've been asked, it's dinner time."

"Thanks." For one pathetic minute, I'm grateful.

"Go over to the door and slide open the hatch next to it. Your food's inside."

I rush over, desperate, only to discover a bowl of grey mush. It looks like thick, lumpy porridge or rotten mashed potato.

"Well?" demands Grinson, his eyes gleaming. "Aren't you going to say thank you?"

"What is it?"

"It's a special mix of nutrients, protein, carbohydrate, vitamins and everything else your body needs to stay alive. Along with some other stuff. Try some."

"I don't have any cutlery," I point out, stalling.

"And you're not getting any. Use your hands."

I scoop some of the wet and sticky goop up with my fingers and slide it into my mouth. It's cold and slimy and I know it won't taste great, but nothing prepares me for just how bad it is. It's like eating salty, soggy cardboard with bits of grit.

I screw up my face with disgust. "I can't eat this. It's rank!"

Grinson smirks. "We came up with that recipe especially for you. It's a shame you don't like it, because that's all you'll get from now on. The same stuff for breakfast, lunch and dinner. Unless you start talking."

I force myself to take another mouthful of the mush, trying to convince myself it isn't so bad. I need to satisfy my hunger. However evil Grinson is, he isn't likely to give me anything poisonous. I'm hoping I'll get used to it with time, but I cough and retch.

My eyes well up with tears.

A wicked smile appears on Grinson's face. "Officer Spencer's going to love this. He suggested we put you on this special diet and asked us to send him the video. I think he's eating steak right now. Anything you want to say to him?"

There are a lot of things I want to say, but it would be a mistake.

Or would it?

I need to rethink my strategy.

Grinson is a mean and nasty individual. He's going to keep moving the goalposts, finding new ways to make me suffer. I stood in the corner for hours and all I've got in return is a bowl of disgusting slop. Whatever I do, he'll never give me screen-time as a reward.

But maybe there's another way...

A plan forms in my mind. It's risky but I can't see any other way out.

If it's going to work, I have to defy Grinson at every opportunity. I need to push every one of his buttons until he hates me. I have to be the worst prisoner he's ever had.

"You can tell Officer Spencer that I hope he chokes on his steak!" I throw the grey mush across the room, splattering it on the wall and floor. "And I hope his arm gets infected where I bit it! I'm not going to follow any more of your stupid rules!"

It's Grinson's turn to be disappointed. "You're going to regret that."

"Not as much as your mum regrets having you! You're a psycho. And just in case no-one's ever told you, you're also the ugliest guy I've ever seen. Have you ever heard of zit-cream? Now, leave me in peace. I'm gonna get some sleep."

Grinson seems lost for words; he opens and closes his mouth like a goldfish. I guess I've hit a nerve with my last insult; he must be self-conscious about his looks. It feels good to score a point over him, but I know I'll pay. After a few seconds, he turns off the screen.

My heart is thudding in my chest. This man can make my life a living hell and I've asked him to do his worst.

But my plan depends on it.

If I'm going to contact the Collective, then I need him to turn on the screen. And if he won't do it to make me happy, maybe he'll do it to cause me pain. It's not foolproof, but it's the best I can come up with in my half-starved condition.

The problem is, there are a lot of other things he can do as well.

And none of them are good.

***

"On your feet." He sounds furious.

I'd be lying if I said I wasn't scared.

But I have to play this cool. I roll over on the bed, but don't make any attempt to get up.

"206, you don't know how much trouble you're in. Don't make it worse on yourself."

"Why, what you gonna do? Are you gonna make me look at your face all day? Cause that is pretty terrifying."

Grinson peers at me, like I'm a bug he's about to squash. "Still the tough guy, huh? Sometime soon, you'll be regretting this. You'll beg for the pain to stop."

"Yeah, well, until then would you mind shutting up?" I stretch and yawn. "I'm trying to sleep here." I roll back to face the wall.

A brief pause. "Sorry for disturbing you. Sweet dreams."

I don't respond.

The silence is worse than the threats. I know he's about to to do something terrible. The only question is what? It doesn't take long to find out.

A blue liquid erupts out of sprinklers in the ceiling, raining down on the room. I jump off the bed, looking for shelter. I pull the blanket over me in an attempt to keep dry but the material is soaking wet in seconds and the liquid drips through. The fluid smells like bathroom cleaner and has a slippery texture. A small stream has formed at the edge of the room, making its way to a small drain in the corner. And still the sprinklers don't stop.

I dive under the desk, sitting in a puddle. I can see Grinson laughing on the screen, enjoying the show. A few seconds later, the sprinklers shut off. I emerge, the damp boiler suit clinging to my body.

"Sorry. Did that disturb you? I thought your room needed a clean, so I turned on the automatic disinfectant system. I didn't mean to wake you."

I stay silent, pretending it doesn't bother me.

"Not got anything to say?" asks Grinson.

"Yeah, are you finished?" I say it with as much disdain as I can manage. "Your whiny voice is so annoying. I don't know how I'm expected to sleep with the constant noise."

"You're not making this easy on yourself," he warns.

"Are you *still* talking," I reply, sounding much more confident than I feel. "What does a guy have to do for some peace around here?"

The screen turns off.

Grinson is bound to be thinking about his next move.

I can only hope that I've dropped enough hints for him to do what I need him to.

This better work, Zac. This better work.

TWENTY-SEVEN

The mattress might be thin and uncomfortable, but it's also waterproof. I guess that's so it doesn't get ruined every time the automatic disinfectant system comes on. By flipping it over, I can lie on the side that's still dry. I can't use the pillow or blanket, though, as they're both soaking wet. I pretend not to care as I curl up on the ledge.

Spending the next sixty days in this room is looking worse and worse. Not only will I be bored, but I'm never going to get any decent food. I wonder how long it will be before I'm so hungry I either rat out the Resistance or have another go at eating the grey mush.

I try to take my mind off it, to think about something else. I wonder if my mum and brother went through anything like this when they were arrested. Layla told me that after quarantine, they'd gone to prison, so even now they're probably in a cell. If so, I hope they still get to see each other. And I hope they don't have anyone as sadistic as Grinson in charge of them. I miss them so much it hurts.

Maybe if I succeed in my mission, I'll be able to get them freed. The thought spurs me on. The Collective need to be defeated, and they need to pay for everything they've done.

"Enjoying the peace and quiet?" I glance up to see Grinson's face on the screen.

"I was," I say, pointedly. "But you had to spoil it, didn't you?"

"As it happens, I've decided that you don't deserve any." Grinson gives a twisted smile. "Instead, you're going to listen to some music."

Grinson's face disappears, but the screen doesn't turn off. Instead, it goes dark blue and a white triangle appears in the centre showing the system is being used to play audio. A couple of seconds later, it starts. It's so loud I think my head is going to explode; a crazy opera duet between a deep-throated man and a very emotional woman. The words are all foreign so I have no idea what they're singing about.

"Turn it off!" I shout over the noise. "Make it stop!"

I lean against the wall, holding my ears, pain and distress on my face. I'm not acting; it's horrific. Grinson will be watching, seeing me squirm.

But there's something he doesn't know: this is exactly what I want him to do. He needs to think that this is the perfect way to break me. I need him to leave the screen on, even if it's just to play music.

He won't know that's any use to me as he's locked me out of the controls.

I have to time this right, else it'll all be for nothing.

That means I have to wait, which isn't easy to do when you're listening to this kind of racket. Even with my hands over my ears, I can hear it. He's set it on an endless repeating loop so I have to listen to the same bit again and again. Even holding out long enough to execute my plan is going to be difficult.

What makes it harder is not knowing how long

I should wait. How will I know when Grinson is watching?

I realise now that this is the biggest flaw in my plan.

And I don't have the answer.

***

For once, my luck is in.

I've been listening to the music for hours, too afraid to make my move. I'm huddled on the bed, the damp pillow pressed over my ears.

The music cuts out and Grinson's face appears.

"Enjoying the music, 206?"

"Please," I say, "no more."

"I'll stop playing it, if you're ready to talk about the Resistance?"

I let out a low moan and shake my head. "I don't know anything."

Grinson leans towards the screen. "I'll let you in on a secret. In ten minutes, I finish my shift, and I head home to my nice *peaceful* house, while you get to stay here. When I go, I can leave the music playing, so you can enjoy it all night long. Maybe you'll remember something you can tell us in the morning, when I'm back?"

My eyes widen in horror. "No," I whisper. "You can't. You can't leave it on that long. I can't take it."

Grinson is enjoying this. "I'm even going to turn off the camera, so the night-shift can't see how much distress you're in. That way, however much you plead or scream or act out, no-one will come to your rescue. For twelve whole hours you're going to suffer and you won't be able to make it stop."

"Anything else," I whine. "Do anything else, but not that!"

He leans back. "There's only one way you can stop it from happening. And this is the last time I'm going to ask before I go: are you ready to tell us about the Resistance?"

I drop to the floor, on to my knees. I need to make this look good. "I'm sorry for what I said earlier, honestly I am. But I can't tell you what I don't know."

"Wrong answer. Perhaps when I come back, you'll be ready to talk. Or maybe you'll learn to *love* opera."

He laughs horribly, then disappears. A few seconds later, the music restarts. Even if you did like that kind of music, the sheer repetitiveness would drive anyone crazy.

I have to give it to him: it's a genius form of torture. If I have to listen to that for the whole night, I'll rip off my own ears. I hope my plan works. If not, I'm about to have the worst night of my life.

But now, I have hope. Grinson has told me what I needed to know. He meant to scare me by telling me he was leaving me alone and no-one could see me. But, it couldn't be more perfect. No-one will be watching me tonight, which gives me the time I need to carry out my plan.

I have the opportunity to try to hack the system.

I just hope I can.

Else it's going to be a very long night.

TWENTY-EIGHT

I rock back and forth on the bed, trying to think about anything but the music.

It's no good rushing this. I have to be sure that Grinson has finished his shift and gone home. When I'm sure I've waited long enough, I make my way over to the wall.

Stodgy grey mush is still splattered across it. I scoop a large glob of the mixture into my hand, then slip off one of the black plimsoll shoes and scrape the gloop onto the rubber sole. I don't want to risk getting electrocuted.

Slowly, I kneel down under the screen and lift the cover of the plug point.

"Here goes nothing," I mutter.

I use the shoe to force the mushy food into the holes of the power socket, keeping the rubber sole between me and the electrical current. If I get this right, the live current will make contact with the earth, and the circuit will trip. Everything will reset when the power comes back on, my screen included. And as Howard taught me, computer systems are always at their weakest when they're booting up.

My first attempts fail. All I manage to do is smear the white plastic with grey mush. I wipe it off with my finger and try again.

This time, as I push the shoe against the power socket, there's a sudden spark, then the smell of burning rubber. All the lights go out. The music stops, replaced by a high-pitched squeal. Either that, or my ears can't cope with the silence.

I sit there, on the floor of my cell, my heart thudding.

If anyone knows what I've done, I'll be in even more trouble than before.

But no-one comes running. There are no angry voices or heavy boots in the corridor. It appears that no-one has even noticed what's happened. I wonder if I'll be sat here all night in the dark. If no-one reboots the system, the plan won't work.

"Come on," I mutter. "This can't be the only room without power."

The darkness is so complete, I can't see my hand in front of my face. I guess I should just be grateful that the music has stopped, but the idea of spending all night like this still doesn't fill me with joy.

There's a whirring sound, and then a click. The lights turn on, almost blinding me. I cover my eyes while they adjust.

As soon as I can bear it, I look at the screen. For the first time, I can see lines of code as the system switches on.

I hold down some keys, praying that the reboot has also reset the keyboard. It has. A blue screen appears before me, giving me access to the registry. From here, I can bypass the usual security protocols. Howard might have worked me hard in my lessons at the pub, but right now, I could kiss him.

Before long, I'm able to open a web browser and log in to Jamie's email account. I had to memorise the details for that back at Resistance HQ. As soon as I'm in, I compose a new message to Jamie's uncle: "Quarantine Agency boarded our boat. Being held in East Anglia Quarantine Centre Room 206. They think I'm part of the Resistance. I haven't told them my name. Anton and Cassandra have also been taken into quarantine. They're trying to interrogate me, making my life hell. Please help. J."

I send it, hoping it will be enough.

The Resistance always spoke as though the Collective were all-powerful and controlled everything in the country from their secret headquarters, but that can't be true. Me, Anton and Cassandra all got arrested and taken into quarantine when we were on our way to Arcadia.

I figure that, like the Resistance, the Collective don't want anyone to know what they're up to. They have to keep their existence a secret. Given that, will they be able to rescue me?

I hope so, else Grinson is going to make mincemeat out of me.

Now, I have another decision to make. Should I also contact the Resistance? They probably think I'd already arrived at Arcadia. I should inform them that hasn't happened.

In one of my long lessons with Howard, he'd shown me how to contact him through an encrypted channel. I use that knowledge now, accessing the BikerLyfe messaging site and requesting an online chat with UserH1097.

Seconds later, Howard's nerdy face pops up on the screen. For once, I'm glad to see him.

"Howard!"

"Zac, what's going on?" Howard looks distracted, probably reading my location data from another of his screens.

"Things didn't go to plan. On the way to Arcadia, I got caught by the Quarantine Agency. I'm being held at the East Anglia Quarantine Centre."

"This is far from ideal." Howard shakes his head, as if it's somehow my fault.

"For what it's worth, I'm not exactly having a great time here. They're torturing me for information about the Resistance. But I've got Net access so I could message the Collective. I'm hoping they'll arrange a rescue."

"Good." He peers at me. "You realise we can't do anything. If we step in, it'll blow your cover."

"I get that. I just wanted to let you know what the situation was, and that there had been a delay. How's everyone else?"

"I don't know," admits Howard. "How should I know?"

I sigh. Of all the people in the Resistance, I get to speak to the one who never leaves his room. "Did everyone get back safely the other night?" I ask, worried about Del and the other bikers.

"Ah, yes. Some bikes were damaged but everyone from this unit returned."

"That's good. How are Kieran and Jamie?"

"Who?"

"Never mind. Do I need to do anything here to cover my tracks? Will they be able to trace this conversation if they double-check the system?"

Howard snorts. "They're the Quarantine Agency, not MI6. They don't have a hope of cracking the encryption we use."

"Well, say hi to everyone from me."

"What? Yes, of course." He won't, though; he's just being polite. But at least he'll pass my update on to Layla, and that's what matters.

"I'd better go." In some ways, I want to talk for longer, but it's a pointless risk, and the conversation is already getting awkward.

"Good luck." Howard ends the call.

I lean back on the bed and pull up the time

display. 10.36pm. Grinson must have ended his shift sometime around 9pm, and he said something about twelve hours off, meaning he's due back at 9am tomorrow. Still, I can't take any chances.

"Computer, set an alarm for 7.50am." I say. The alarm will remind me to start the opera music playing before Grinson returns. Hopefully, he'll think I've had to endure it all night, and he won't know I've hacked the system.

I spend the next few hours watching TV, trying to distract myself from my empty stomach.

How long will it take for the Collective to get my message and take some action? The thought of even a few more days of Grinson's torture fills me with dread.

Tough it out, Zac.

I lie down on the hard, uncomfortable mattress and try to sleep.

TWENTY-NINE

The alarm sounds.

Somehow, despite having no pillow or blanket and the hardest bed ever, I've slept through the night. Probably due to sheer exhaustion.

I stretch and sit up, enjoying the silence. It can't last long. I know what I have to do.

Slowly, I head over to the keyboard, then spend some time double-checking that the system looks exactly like Grinson left it. The last thing I do is restart the terrible opera music.

Hopefully, Grinson will have no idea that I haven't endured the onslaught for the entire night. I shudder as I imagine what that would have been like, and how close I came to that terrible fate. If my plan hadn't worked, I'd be going crazy right now.

Even listening to it for an hour is torture. Grinson doesn't appear for ages. When his face shows up on the screen, he smiles to see me curled up on the bed, my hands pressed to my ears. I've rubbed my eyes red and make sure that I look tired and scared, as if I've been through hell.

"Had a good night's sleep?" he mocks. "Enjoying the music?"

"Make it stop!" I plead. "I can't take it."

Grinson silences the music and looks at me lying pathetically on the bed.

"Hungry?" he asks.

I nod. I don't even need to pretend about that. My stomach is so empty it hurts.

"Breakfast is ready. Why don't you fetch it?" An evil smile stretches across his thin lips. I know what to expect as I open the hatch. Sure enough, another bowl of the grey sludge is waiting for me. I'm so desperate for something to eat that I'm willing to give it another go. I take a small scoop in my fingers and force it into my mouth.

"You seem a lot less cocky this morning," observes Grinson. "Imagine what you'll be like after a few more days listening to that."

I look up at him, my eyes wide. "Please. Don't do it. I'll be good, I promise."

"Having any regrets about all the things you said?"

"Yes," I admit. "I'm sorry. I won't act up again."

"Well, actions have consequences. So, this morning you're going to do a bit of exercise."

"How?" I ask, surprised. The room is way too small for that.

"Let's have two hundred press ups for a start." He grins, enjoying his power. "You can do them in sets of twenty."

I open my mouth to object but realise that if I complain, he'll probably double it.

"This is only your second day here. Are you sure you don't remember anything about the Resistance?"

"I told you, I don't know anything."

"Well, then, you better start your press-ups."

I leave the food on the bed and drop to the floor. I manage the first forty easily, but the next twenty are a struggle and I only just get them done before I collapse.

After a short rest, I get back into position and

try again, sweat forming on my forehead.

Grinson is going to play his little games with me every day, and I can't do anything about it. Except hope for a rescue.

***

"Enjoying yourself, 206?"

I've managed over a hundred and twenty press-ups but my arms are shaking. There's no way I'm going to get to two hundred.

"I can't do any more." I roll on to my side.

"Hmmm. You look hot. Perhaps I can help cool you down."

He reaches forward and presses a button. The sprinkler system bursts into life, droplets of cold blue liquid falling from the ceiling. I crawl towards the desk for shelter.

"No, 206. Stay where you are. You don't get to hide. You have some press-ups to finish, unless you'd rather listen to some delightful music?"

Anything but that.

I stretch back out on the floor. The slimy disinfectant runs through my hair and soaks into my clothing. My tired arms scream at me to stop but I keep pushing on, barely able to make five more push-ups. I'm not tough enough to take this. I collapse on the ground. Tears run down my cheeks, mixing with the liquid as it drips off my face.

Eventually, the sprinklers stop, but my tears don't.

"Still not ready to talk?" Grinson examines his nails as if he couldn't care less. If I say no, he'll carry on with this torture. Hour after hour, day after day.

I'll crack, eventually.

Just give in.

What's the point of holding out any longer? Grinson is just going to find new ways to cause me pain. Or he'll keep playing the music, which is even worse.

But what can I tell him that will make him stop?

Maybe I can come up with something like they want to hear, but mix it with enough lies to keep my friends in the Resistance safe? I don't know if it will work, but it has to be better than this.

I open my mouth to speak.

Suddenly, everything goes dark, just like when

I tripped the electrics.

With no windows, I can't see a thing. I'm not sure if someone else has shorted the system or whether Grinson has cut off the power.

I sit up and hug my legs, wondering when this nightmare will be over.

A few minutes pass.

What's happening?

The door bursts open. Light from the corridor spills into the room.

Grinson is standing there, dressed in a full hazmat suit, his blotchy face redder than ever behind the plastic visor.

"What did you do?" he demands.

"Nothing." It's the truth. Unless some of the gunk is still stuck in the plug, I didn't do anything to cause this power cut.

He walks towards me and I scurry backwards on my hands and knees until I collide with the wall.

"There's nowhere to run," he sneers. "And in here, no-one can hear you scream."

This guy has lost it. The Quarantine Agency might allow him some slack in the way he carries out his job, but there's no way they'd let him assault a kid.

"You'll get into trouble. I'll report you."

"You won't dare."

I'm shaking now, wondering what he has planned. "I didn't do anything. You were watching on the screen. I was lying on the floor."

As if to prove my innocence, at that moment, the power comes back on. The room is flooded with light. That doesn't seem to make any difference to Grinson.

"Get up."

I scramble to my feet, and consider my options.

I could hit him. Or even better, I could kick him in the groin.

But what would be the point? It would give me some satisfaction, sure. But even if I got into the corridor, I'd never get through all the locked gates.

Besides, any hope of escape disappears a few seconds later. Over Grinson's shoulder, I can see two more QA officers entering my room, dressed in full protective gear. Maybe they're here to help Grinson? Or perhaps I can at least get them to intervene?

"Help!" I cry out to them. "This guy is crazy. He's gone mad."

Even through the visor, I can see Grinson is confused. He glances behind, to see who I'm speaking with. He's surprised to see anyone else there. "Can I help you, officers? It appears you're in the wrong room."

"No, we're definitely in the right room," says one of the visitors. "Jamie, you need to come with us."

It takes me a few seconds to work out what they've said.

"Who are you?" I ask.

This time, the other one speaks. "Your uncle sent us."

It's too good to be true. "What about Anton and Cassandra?"

"They're coming too. We have to move."

"You can't take this boy anywhere," objects Grinson. "He's in quarantine."

"I think you'll find we can." The man points a gun at him. Now it's Grinson's turn to cower in the corner. "You stay there, and don't move. Jamie, let's go."

"Wait, there's something I need to do. It'll only

take a minute." I head over to the keyboard, and start tapping away.

"That won't work. I disabled..." Grinson trails off, shocked to see I have control of the system. "How did you do that?"

"That doesn't matter. All that matters is that you get a taste of your own medicine."

"What do you mean?"

"Let's just say, I hope you like opera." The music starts up, even louder than before. Grinson can't even cover his ears with his visor on. "Can we lock him in?" I ask my rescuers. "He deserves to suffer."

"I can't see why not." The man shepherds me out of the door.

Grinson edges towards the keyboard. He's hoping he can override the commands and get a message to his colleagues.

"Good luck with that," I say. "I've disabled it. Properly this time."

"You can't leave me here," he yells, over the racket. "It'll be hours before anyone finds me."

I glare at him, my eyes cold. "I hope it's days." With that, I pull the door shut. "How do I lock it?"

"It's automatic. Can't be opened from the inside. Come on, we've wasted enough time as it is."

We jog down corridors, my rescuers leading the way. Whenever we reach a security door, the woman scans a card, and it lets us through.

We head up a flight of stairs and out an emergency exit into the blinding sun. A minibus is parked nearby. The woman jumps in the back and beckons me to follow. Anton and Cassandra are sat in the seats opposite.

"Hey!" I say, as I clamber in.

Cassandra beams at me. "Jamie! You made it! And somehow you got us rescued!"

"We owe you one," agrees Anton, ruffling my hair.

I shrug. "I only sent a message. We have to thank my uncle for this."

"Don't worry," laughs Cassandra. "We will."

With a roar of the engine and a squeal of tyres, we're off.

THIRTY

The minibus speeds down country roads, leaving the quarantine centre far behind.

"Why are you so wet?" asks Cassandra.

"It's disinfectant." I run my hand through my soaking hair. "This officer called Grinson kept turning on the sprinklers in my room."

"No way! That can't be legal."

"I tried telling him that. But because I wouldn't tell them anything about the Resistance, he seemed to think I was fair game. Did they do the same to you?"

"They kept asking questions." Cassandra shudders and looks away. "They made a lot of threats. Probably just trying to scare us, but I think it was about to get worse."

My damp clothes stick to me as I fidget in the

seat, but the sun is shining through the windows. I'll soon dry.

The couple who rescued me are taking off their visors. One of them is a woman, who gives me a warm smile. "Hi Jamie, I'm Rachel. Are you ok?"

"I'm alright now I'm out of that place," I say, gruffly. "Except they didn't feed me anything. Is there any food?"

The man in the passenger seat rustles around in the glove compartment and hands me a cereal bar. I tear off the wrapper and wolf it down.

Cassandra looks worried. "You really are starving."

"It's only a couple of hours to Arcadia," soothes Rachel. "As soon as we get there, we'll sort you out with a proper meal."

As far as I'm concerned, that can't come soon enough.

"We'll be at a checkpoint in a few minutes," warns the driver. He uses his free hand to pull on a hood with a visor, like the Quarantine Agency officers wear.

"Here, put this on." Rachel hands me one of my own. I reluctantly pull it over my head. It feels hot and oppressive. Inside the mask, the air tastes of metal and my visor steams up every time I take a breath. Peering through the fog, I can see the others have done the same.

Up ahead are the red and white barriers and small booths of a lockdown checkpoint. We're the only vehicle out here—the whole road is deserted.

A guard looks out of his booth and peers through the minibus windows. He communicates with our driver through an intercom.

"Please state the reason for your journey," he says, robotically.

Our driver does a good job of sounding bored. "Transfer of patients to Vicron-X Research Centre. Here's the paperwork."

He holds up some official-looking documents. The guard glances at them through his small window. "We don't usually have Quarantine Agency transfers through here."

"We rarely have to take them this far," agrees the driver. "Who knows what they need these three for. Apparently, they have some special genetic sequencing that might help with developing a vaccine, but to be honest it's above my pay grade."

The guard seems to relax. "Well, let's hope they do some good. That vaccine can't come soon enough."

He presses a button, and the barrier raises up, allowing us through. As soon as the checkpoint is out of sight, we pull off the oppressive masks.

I breathe a sigh of relief. "I can't believe some people have to wear these things all day. How do they cope? I'd die."

Cassandra laughs. "Sounds like they should have made you wear one of those in quarantine. You might have told them everything."

I smile and shake my head. "Nah. It wouldn't have worked. I don't rat on anyone. Ever." I don't tell them how close I'd come to breaking under Grinson's torture.

Anton looks impressed. "Your uncle is going to be proud."

The mention of my uncle reminds me why I'm here. I'm so happy to have escaped quarantine, I've almost forgotten about my mission. I already think of Cassandra and Anton as friends, but I have to betray them. I'm going into Arcadia as a spy to bring the Collective down.

A pang of guilt mixes with my hunger.

I try to push it to the back of my mind.

***

I jerk awake when someone shouts: "We're here!"

We're driving through dense forest, the sun glinting through the leaves above. The road is little more than a dirt track through the undergrowth. The minibus steers left, taking us along the shore of a sparkling blue lake. I stare at it, mesmerised by its beauty after the cold grey walls of quarantine.

Cassandra puts her hand on my shoulder. "I let you sleep for as long as I could, even when we came through the gates, but I thought you'd want to see this."

She points out the other side of the minibus. I gasp as I turn to see stunning buildings of glass, wood and metal rising among the trees. The biggest of them are on the ground, but some cling to solid trunks like futuristic treehouses, connected to everything else with neat wooden walkways.

"It's incredible," I murmur. I've seen pictures of Arcadia but they didn't prepare me for this. The minibus stops in a small clearing and we climb out.

"Come with me," says Rachel.

I follow her towards a nearby building. Its front is a wall of glass. All I can see in it is a reflection of the surrounding forest and the blue sky.

As we approach, doors slide open and someone steps out: a man with a slim build and a handsome face. I know who he is: it's a face I've seen before on a file in the Resistance headquarters.

"Hi Jamie, I'm your Uncle Aaron. Welcome to Arcadia."

I force a smile and step forward. "It's good to finally meet you, Uncle."

We embrace awkwardly, then he grips my shoulders and looks into my eyes. I feel exposed, as though he can read my mind. He's sharp and focused, and I wonder if he already knows I'm an imposter.

If he does, he doesn't let on. "I hear it's been a pretty arduous trip. But you can forget about that now. You're here and you're safe. Your new life can begin."

I feel like he wants me to say something epic, but there's only one thing that's on my mind. "Can I have something to eat? I'm starving."

He laughs. "We can arrange that."

He ushers me along the walkway and I take my first steps into a new world.

EPILOGUE

And now?

Now I'm here, in the most beautiful place I've ever seen. If I'm honest, the Resistance, my mission, the real reason I'm here all seem so far away, like something from a past life.

This is a refreshing and hopeful place. The people are friendly. It's difficult to believe that they're responsible for keeping the country in lockdown.

It's hard to imagine they're evil.

Are the Resistance wrong about the Collective?

Or am I being naïve.

I have to find out, and fast.

The Resistance are counting on me to bring the whole thing crashing down. But I don't know if I can.

Truthfully, I'm not sure that I want to.

It's not an easy decision to make. Whatever I do, I end up betraying someone.

My name is Zac, but nobody knows that.

Sometimes, I even forget it myself.

FIND OUT WHAT HAPPENS NEXT:

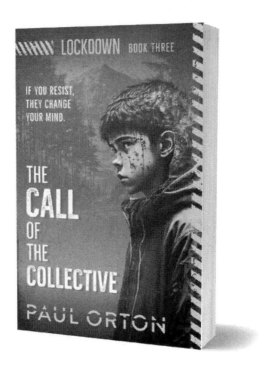

They're selfish and cruel.

That's what he was told.

But the more time Zac spends with the Collective, the more he has his doubts. How could these people be responsible for the lockdown? Why would they suppress a vaccine?

He has to get answers, and fast.

He's meant to be a Resistance spy, not a child of the Collective. This is no time to question his orders and betray his friends. He needs to stay focused and complete his mission.

If he doesn't, it will all be for nothing.

And the lockdown will never end.

Want to know when it's released? Sign up to my reader's club for updates, free books and more!

Check out <u>www.paulorton.net</u> for more details.

A NOTE FROM THE AUTHOR

Thanks for reading *The Rise of the Resistance*. I'll soon be releasing the next book in the Lockdown series: *The Call of the Collective*. If you want to be kept informed when it's released then check out www.paulorton.net.

You may also want to get hold of my other books: the *Ryan Jacobs* series. If you like teenagers with attitude, you'll love Ryan Jacobs! You can even download the prequel to the series completely free on my website.

But first, could you do me a huge favour? I'd love you to review *The Rise of the Resistance* on Amazon. Reviews make a huge difference to an independent author like me, and it would be amazing if you could write a sentence or two about what you liked about it. I'd really appreciate it and I promise I read every review.

Until next time,

Paul.

GET YOUR FREE EBOOK

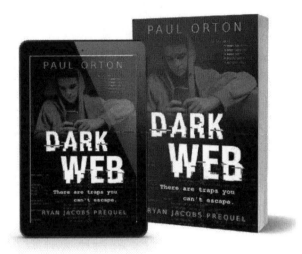

There are traps you can't escape.

When Ryan Jacobs asks to join the Faction he finds himself trapped in a situation which keeps getting worse. He needs to escape fast, or they will own him forever. But how can he fight an invisible enemy?

Find out about Ryan's life before he is taken to the Academy. DARK WEB is exclusively available to those in my readers' club – sign up for free at www.paulorton.net

RYAN JACOBS BOOK 1

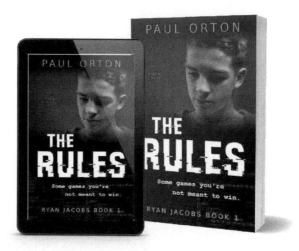

Somehow, he lost his freedom.

Now he belongs to the Academy, and the rules have changed. What started out as a game has become a matter of life and death.

If he doesn't think fast, someone will die.

At thirteen you shouldn't have to face these kinds of issues. But at thirteen, you don't get to decide the rules.

THE RULES is the first book in the Ryan Jacobs series and is <u>AVAILABLE NOW ON AMAZON</u>!

RYAN JACOBS BOOK 2

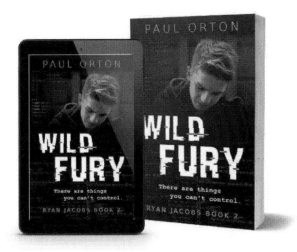

They call it the Fury. And no-one is safe.

Life has got very complicated for Ryan. The fact is that he's never been much of a team player. It's not easy when your friends hate you and everyone else is on your case.

And that was before people started going crazy. He has to find some answers, and fast. Before things get out of hand. Before anyone gets killed. Or worse.

WILD FURY is the second book in the Ryan Jacobs series and is <u>AVAILABLE NOW ON AMAZON!</u>

RYAN JACOBS BOOK 3

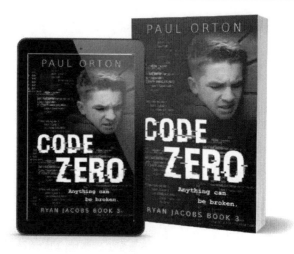

There's something in the woods.
And it's out of control.

When Ryan realises the danger, he has a difficult decision to make: it's not easy to own up to your mistakes when you're already in so much trouble. But if he doesn't, someone could die.

Will he be able to tame the technology before anyone is killed? Or will he confess and lose his place at the academy? At thirteen, it's a harsh choice. But, this time, he only has himself to blame.

CODE ZERO is the third book in the Ryan Jacobs series and is <u>AVAILABLE NOW ON AMAZON</u>!

RYAN JACOBS BOOK 4

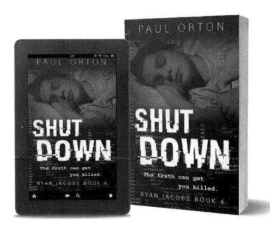

Everyone has secrets.
Even those you least expect.

Ryan is in trouble. He has to stop the shutdown but doesn't know who to trust. The authorities are closing in and he's running out of time. It's not easy being thirteen and having a reputation. Whatever he does, his enemies are one step ahead.

Will he uncover the truth? And will anyone believe him if he does?

SHUT DOWN is the fourth book in the Ryan Jacobs series and is <u>AVAILABLE NOW ON AMAZON</u>!

Printed in Great Britain
by Amazon

35115853R00135